The Ghosts of Smyrna

a novel

Loren Edizel

We acknowledge the support of the Canada Council for the Arts for our publishing program. We also acknowledge support from the Government of Ontario through the Ontario Arts Council.

We acknowledge the financial support of the Government of Canada through the Canada Book Fund for our publishing activities.

 Canada Council   Conseil des Arts   ONTARIO ARTS COUNCIL
for the Arts   du Canada   CONSEIL DES ARTS DE L'ONTARIO   Canada

Cover design by Ingrid Paulson
Photograph of the author by Edwin Gailits

Edizel, Loren, author
        The ghosts of Smyrna : a novel / Loren Edizel.

        ISBN 978-1-927494-22-6 (pbk.)

I. Title.

Printed and bound in Canada by Coach House Printing

TSAR Publications
P. O. Box 6996, Station A
Toronto, Ontario M5W 1X7
Canada

www.tsarbooks.com

To the memory of Jak Edizel,
my beloved father

To Kamhi,
With my best wishes,
love Edzel
Nov. 14, 2013

Contents

Aya Katerina

Smyrna in the Ottoman Empire, at the end of World War I. Niko would remember a hand-painted sepia postcard from his aunt's collection. She had a wooden box full of postcards, some given to her and others bought, from which she sometimes drew inspiration to paint. In this one, a florid hand-written *Bienvenue à Smyrne* formed an arc at the top of the picture, which depicted a milkman and his faithful ass on a narrow cobblestone street at midday. Niko always thought of this as the picture of silence itself, punctuated by the occasional wail of a child or the abrupt closing of shutters at the noon hour. On both sides of the road slumbering houses leaned on each other, their windows darkened by the Ottoman kafes, wooden cagelike screens to protect women from curious eyes and from the sight of the outside world coming in at once. Only little diamonds at a time.

He tried to spy on the street, without being noticed, an eye or two peeping out from the kafes. A girl's eye, perhaps, or a grandmother's. He imagined statuesque females at different stages of life, wrapped in black sheets from head to toe, nibbling absentmindedly on baklava, watching the world pass by. He saw a girl looking out once. He was returning from school, walking on the narrow pavement. He looked up and saw two eyes blink at him. They slanted into a smile. Pink fingertips stuck out of the openings and wiggled. He felt an uncontrollable desire to pull on all those pink digits, but

1

simply stuck his tongue out in greeting and walked on.

Aya Katerina, was a Rum* neighbourhood, named after the church in its midst. The inhabitants were mostly Orthodox, but there were Jews, Moslems, Catholics, and Armenians as well, and they mostly communicated in Romeika, a Smyrnian version of Greek, mixed with Italian, Turkish, and God knew what else. Sturdy women in calico aprons talked loudly to each other as they vigorously beat the balding carpets wagging from balconies like brightly coloured tongues. No kafeses. Big white boxers on clotheslines blowing in the breeze, brassieres swelling up. The only man on the street was Toothless Ahmet, the milkman, whose donkey, Five Legs, had a permanent erection, not apparent on the postcard. The other man was inside the house—Niko's Uncle Polycarp who hadn't been drafted. All the others were fighting the war. On the street, Niko was sometimes General Liman, a German with a monocle, walking with a limp to appear more heroic. On the British side they called him General Lemon which only made their predicament worse. Everyone else called him the Orphan. He lived with his grand-mother, uncle, and Aunt Elena in a white two-storey house with green shutters.

His grandmother Marie told him the story of how he became the Orphan. One day she received a condolence letter from the Sultan himself, when Niko was three years of age, declaring his father a shehit, a fallen soldier. It explained in respectful and ornate lan-guage that he had died fighting the Arabs in Damascus. The Arabs had Lawrence. His father had dysentery. It could not be helped. A monthly golden lira was awarded to his grandmother to raise the Orphan. This was read to her by the neighbour Emine Hanım, who translated it into Romeika for her. In the entire neighbour-hood, only Emine Hanım could read the Arabic script. The story went that she was the daughter of an Ottoman pasha, raised in

*Anatolian Greek

affluence, thus was able to read and write.

Nowadays she beat her own carpets while shouting greetings across the alley because she could not afford a maid. Her husband sold spices in a small store on Frenk Sokağı.* In the evenings, when he walked by, the smell of oregano and cumin made you dream of grilled lamb meat. The kids had nicknamed him Köfte.** When she was sixteen, Emine eloped with Köfte before they could marry her off to one of her father's withered cronies. She was disowned by her family but never looked back.

The young lovers had wandered like gypsies all around Anatolia and the Balkans before settling in Smyrna to hide from her brothers who had vowed to kill them both. No one came looking for them. But they never dared have children, so as not to orphan them in case her brothers succeeded in their mission. And so they grew old in Aya Katerina. All the children in the neighbourhood knew where to go for candy or have their bicycles repaired.

Emine Hanım finished reading the Sultan's condolence letter, her voice quavering. After listening to the entire letter quietly, Marie's body started shaking with a silent sob that slowly twisted itself and got jammed in her lungs. It stayed there for many years, thinning her hair and twisting her backbone, until it finally left her body with her last breath, as a blood-curdling howl.

*Rue de France
** meatball

Magnetic Forces

FOR A LONG TIME Niko thought the Orphan was his uncle until
one day a lady pointed at him and said, "Aman Allah! How the
Orphan has grown . . . "

It was then that he realized he himself was the famous Orphan,
and no one spoke about Uncle Polycarp. No one spoke to him,
anyway. Uncle must have been in his late thirties then. A wiry
man with a scraggly beard, intensely bulbous eyes, and elongated
hands. He always wore blue-grey striped pyjamas at home. He
hardly ever left the house.

His room smelled a little of rotten apples and coffee, and the
pages of the hundreds of books on his shelves had turned brown.
Niko's room being adjacent to his, he could hear him pace up and
down for hours at night, mumbling or reciting things. His name
came from the patron saint of Smyrna, who was burned alive by
the Romans for preferring Christianity. Polycarp might have had
similar aspirations as his namesake—reaching for unfamiliar ter-
ritory, uncharted thoughts—when tragedy befell him. One morning, before drinking his Turkish coffee, he walked out of the house
in his striped pyjamas and started lecturing Toothless Ahmet's
unsuspecting donkey.

"There are magnets and magnetic forces all around us. I am
made of them and so are you. They attract, they repel. So do people, events, so does time and space. History is made of such forces,

you understand . . . There is no such thing as coincidence."

The sky was Smyrna blue that day, extending from one edge of the universe to the other. Summer heat radiated from the whitewashed wall beside Polycarp towards the street. Toothless Ahmet shyly approached Polycarp who went on,

"If there is no such thing as coincidence, everything in the universe has a reason to be. Not a purpose, but a reason! That is where we must begin . . . Or is it the other way around? Everything in the universe has a purpose but no reason. Purpose with no reason. Reason with no purpose. Reason . . . no purpose. Purpose . . . no reason. Which one? Reason. Purpose. Which one?"

Toothless Ahmet was a polite peasant; he hardly ever looked up when he poured the two frothy litres of milk into the copper pot extended to him by a customer. And now, he didn't know what to do to end his donkey's interrogation. Five Legs, on the other hand, seemed mesmerized by the elongated fingers drawing frantic ellipses in the air.

"Excuse me, hodja," said Toothless Ahmet. "The donkey must go. I'll bring him again tomorrow if you please. Good bye. Good bye." He nodded, eyes downcast, as he led the donkey out of the way. Off they went, leaving Polycarp in the middle of the road, his long hands reaching for his head in confusion. Niko's grandmother came and took her son's elbow and walked him back to the house.

Polycarp slumped into a chair in the kitchen and was silent for a long time. The doctor was brought. He listened to his chest and checked his ears, asked him who he was and made him do a few mental calculations before declaring him sane and sound. He explained that it was momentary confusion, perhaps brought on by the anxiety of war. Warplanes went roaring daily over the city. It was impossible to ignore the paraplegic veterans begging for food on sidewalks. Hospitals were full, supplies were low. The doctor said he sometimes felt like talking to donkeys himself; at least they appeared to listen.

"How come you were not drafted, son?" he asked Polycarp.

"They said I was not fit to join," Polycarp replied slowly, looking down. The doctor looked up at Marie.

"He's always been fragile," she explained.

"Ah," said the doctor, "I see. It's a blessing in disguise, though; at least you have your son beside you instead of lying wounded in some trench."

Marie's face changed; her eyes looked like they needed to escape from their sockets, not knowing where to go. He understood.

"I'm sorry," he apologized. "I'm so sorry, you've already lost one," he said and picked up his hat.

A Dangerous Name

NIKO'S MOTHER HAD DIED at childbirth. He was her first-born and claimed her life for his. The only person who could have told the boy about her habits, how she held her head or laughed, if she was funny or thoughtful, was his father, who was taken away when Niko was very young. His grandmother did not talk much about either of them. Niko kept their pictures under his pillow when he went to sleep. Some nights he held his father's picture in his palm until sleep made him release his grip, and it dropped under the bed. This photograph was signed "Rivoli" in small letters at the bottom left corner. In it his father appeared fair, with a large forehead over bushy eyebrows and light eyes. He had a thick blond moustache, an elegant nose, and full lips, all on a square face sitting on broad shoulders. It was the eyes his son loved the most. They had a liquid, melancholic look as though he had known something all along and was waiting for it to happen.

Easter 1915 or 1916, he no longer remembered exactly. Marie had been roasting the leg of lamb all morning, filling the house with the fragrance of garlic and meat and bay leaves. Little Niko, in his navy blue Sunday suit that she had bought at Peregrini's, was running between the kitchen and the living room, shrieking with delighted fear at the top of his lungs as Polycarp chased him, growling like a wild beast. Elena played the piano accompanied by Jacob, who sang Greek love songs in his velvety baritone voice.

7

The Easter pititzes* were carefully piled on a large plate, to be eaten after lunch, accompanied by a Turkish coffee and a glass of water.

Marie called everyone to the table. There was lamb and red wine. All was well and laughter was easy. A knock on the door. And another. It was not one they recognized. It had a crisp, menacing manner and the house seemed to shake. Marie's heart filled with dread as she rose from her seat. She looked at her children, then at the door, and walked slowly towards it. Gendarmes stood there, bayonets on their rifles, and they showed her some papers. She nodded, partly turned around, shrinking visibly. Outside on the street she could see other people also surrounded by gendarmes. She recognized some of the faces, they were Armenians.

"Which one of you is Jacob Deveciyan?" asked one of the gendarmes at the door.

"I am," Jacob responded and rose, placing his folded napkin on the table.

He was ordered to follow them immediately.

"Where are we going?" he asked feebly.

"To Syria. You will board the train in a few hours."

"Let me pack his belongings . . . " started Marie.

"It will not be necessary," cut in the gendarme. "He will be provided with what he needs."

Jacob's hands were trembling as he hugged his family and finally his young son. Each one of them felt from this hug that there would never be another one. The gendarmes took him away.

Marie put together some pititzes in a napkin and fresh water in a bottle, and they took a coach to the train station in Halkapınar in the hopes of seeing Jacob one more time. They did. He was on the train, bare-chested and in boxers, along with hundreds of other men. They had been made to undress before boarding. Mounds of clothing were on the platform, guarded by soldiers. He waved when he saw them.

*cookies

He hung down to take the pititzes and the water bottle. His son was sitting on Polycarp's shoulders. He managed to ruffle his hair and caress his cheek with his fingertips as the train started moving.

"Why did you take your shirt off, Papa?" asked Niko.

"I'm feeling hot," he replied tenderly, "don't worry."

As the train pulled out of Halkapınar Station they heard him shout, "The boy . . . Mama . . . Protect my boy!" Then he was heard no more.

They waited for news from Damascus, where Jacob and the others were supposedly fighting a war against the Arabs. Did the Arabs know who was coming at them? Jacob had heard various versions of his name. The Italians called him "Devisani," the French "Devision," the Greeks "Devetziannis," and the Ottomans "Deveci-yan." The danger lay in the Ottoman version, which meant he was Armenian and therefore a potential enemy of the State. The timing of the war in Damascus coincided with the political decision to persecute, exile and eliminate Armenians from Eastern Anatolia, because they wished to declare their independence from a crumbling Ottoman Empire. Was he murdered on that fictitious trip to Damascus? Was he used as a soldier in the desperate and losing war against the British and Arabs in Syria? A friend of the family who returned from Damascus said he saw Jacob in a hospital there, being treated for dysentery. Perhaps he invented the story out of pity for the grieving family. Did he die of dysentery? Was he shot in the back for being Armenian? Did an Arab decapitate him for being Ottoman?

Dysentery in uniform was the cause of death chosen by Niko, in whose dreams Jacob lay in soiled green trousers and muddy boots on a hospital bed with off-white metal bars. His head was bandaged, his blond moustache rigid with caked blood and sweat. His naked arms were milky white from shoulder to elbow and tanned from there down. Reddish hair glistening with sweat in the gentle fold of an armpit. His eyes were closed. A portly, thin-lipped French nun in swishing white robes walked towards his bed holding a bedpan and a rosary. "Monsieur Devision . . . Monsieur Devision?" The curtain fell.

Elena, Jacob's sister, was haunted by a different dream night after night. Jacob was in a desert, the midday sun beating on his naked body as he stood inside a crater he had dug with dozens of others. The train could be seen in the dusty background. Soldiers placed around the crater started shooting at the naked men. Jacob looked around as his fellow prisoners fell around him, their eyes wide open, blood pouring out of their mouths, bare legs twitching. There was no mercy in this dream. Her brother looked straight at her, still standing, blood gushing out of his chest. "My boy, Elena, you must take care of my boy." His lips were not moving. It seemed as though his voice was seeping out of his eyes into her head. She awoke screaming.

Jacob had been forewarned. Before he was taken, Elise, an Assyrian lady who helped him at his hat store, had begged him to go into hiding. He started hearing vague, disquieting stories. Neighbours came to tell him about men being spirited away in other districts, sometimes in the middle of the night. His mother begged him to escape. He laughed, refusing to believe his name could be a death warrant. He lived in Smyrna after all, the city where many identities, religions, and languages coexisted. Here you could start a sentence in one language, finish it in another, and no one would think it odd. Although mixed marriages were not common, it was not so unheard of to be a Moslem whose grandmother was Jewish, to be called Achilles with a father named Ahmet, to be a Patterson and have Armenian ancestry. As he was marched through the narrow streets of Aya Katerina, he looked at the gendarme walking beside him, thinking he looked no less Armenian than any of the people being marched towards the train station. But he probably had a safe name to call his own.

Before the war, it had seemed that family names only mattered to the rich and powerful. No one else cared. One was Ali the tailor, Yanni the tavern-keeper, Jacob the milliner. The tragedy over Jacob's name meant that times had changed. Names were now invented, altered, scrutinized and pursued because they meant everything.

Ghosts and Myths

AFTER JACOB'S DISAPPEARANCE, Polycarp withdrew into a world of his own. Elena, on the other hand, was spending more time painting and drawing than she ever did before. What used to be a desultory hobby turned into an obsession. She painted relentlessly, from the moment she woke till the last rays of the sun gave in to darkness. Everything else she did seemed like an afterthought. She painted kettles, members of her family, bowls of fruit, dusty attics, chairs, strangers, seascapes, the port, the market, the Quay. She did not paint her brother Jacob. She could not bring herself to represent the core of her heartache; his beloved face, her nightmares. Instead, she imbued everything she painted with a kind of loving despair that made an old green chair speak more of whomever was no longer seated there, than of itself, thus leaving the viewer with the uneasy sensation of having profoundly misinterpreted the visible world. Her kettles looked more like her mother's calloused hands than kettles, her mother seemed more like an open window on a rainy day than herself. One could almost smell things in her charcoal drawings and watercolours; the resin of a pine tree bulging from the bark, the old, partly disemboweled pink cushion with gold trimmings that lay on the sofa with a confusion of hair and neck odours, the salty sea drops that hit your face when you walked along the Quay on summer afternoons when the imbat started blowing.

Niko knew that a ghost lurked in her paintings. He spent many hours quietly watching her in the stuffy attic, hoping his father would reveal himself through the paint tubes and brushes, in the smell of turpentine and oils on discarded rags. Most of the time she was not even aware of his presence. He watched her from a distance, as always, for one was always watching Elena from a distance, even when sitting on her lap.

In one of her numerous portraits of Polycarp he sits in what appears to be the backyard of the house with a green shrub to his right and a discoloured wooden table to his left. The shadow cast by the kitchen window, left ajar, crosses his face diagonally. He is looking away, yet his gaze is not focused in any particular direction, somewhat in the way an infant's gaze may be captured in photographs, but with the disconsolate gravity of a person who has grown weary of seeking answers. On the table is a pot of basil, the kind with tiny leaves that grow into balls. You could run your hands over it, caressing the leaves, and smell the fragrance filling your palm. Also on the table, next to him, is a bowl of peas half-shelled. He could sit for hours and prepare vegetables for Marie. On the ground, a sleeping dog. One of those quiet, sultry summer afternoons in Smyrna. Time runs thickly, and there is no escaping the passing minutes. They grasp one another until they reach the moment you have barely left behind. Then, all the time spent attaches itself to your future like the tentacles of a medusa. In Smyrna, time stings. Polycarp thought so. He once told his nephew that the secret of eternity rested in Smyrna. "How so?" asked the boy.

"Once upon a time," started Polycarp, "Keros was flying over the city on one of his regular runs, checking up on people and pursuing those who tried to escape him. He sped on his fluffy cloud with his eyes fixed on the Aegean coast. Of all the regions in the world, this was the place that drove him insane. Why? Because Aegeans ignored him completely no matter what he did. Keros appeared to them as a minor annoyance, hard as he tried to convince them otherwise. It bruised his pride to remain unacknowledged on his panoply of clouds while he worked so hard to make sure everything happened on time. He much preferred the yodeling barbarians in the deep and mountainous regions of Europe (before it was called Europe). They worshipped him. This of course was long before Artemis, Appollo, and Aphrodite, and so on. They were around, to be sure, but under different names and they weren't so narcissistic in those very ancient days as they later became in Homer's time. But that is another story . . . He knew he was not welcome down there among humans, although the gods of the region never failed to prepare a feast in his honour, upon his passage.

"On his way to one of those heavenly feasts, he noticed a dark spot flying faster than the wind along the ivory-coloured beach that stretched for miles and miles. He couldn't make out what it was, and his curiosity made him forget that the gods were waiting, and that he was running late. He swooped down and at first saw the figure of a warrior seated on a horse. His abundant curly hair was flowing down to his waist. How strange, he thought, that a warrior should have such long hair. He leaned forward, and that is when his eyes beheld the loveliest maiden in the world. He dipped down even farther to take a closer look. His cloud was hovering just above her head, moving at the same speed as her horse, which was black as squid ink. She slowed down and looked up in wonder at this strange cloud following her. She did not see him, no one could see Keros but the gods. But, oh, when he saw her face lifted towards the sun, he almost fell off his cloud. This lovely maiden was Queen . Smyrna (who founded the city some four thousand years ago), the one-breasted Amazon queen riding her horse along the beach, carrying her spears and arch on her back. She was built like a man; muscular legs and arms, broad shoulders. She had fought many wars on her way down from the Black Sea and across the plains of Anatolia. Her beauty was energetic, for there was nothing dainty about her countenance. Amazons had only one breast. The left one. The right one was done away with during puberty, to enable them to use their arches without the encumbrance of a breast getting in the way. Unless, of course, they were left-handed.

"When she came to the hills of Bayrakli with her army and saw the turquoise bay meeting the white sandy beaches in the distance, and olive trees with cicadas buzzing away, she turned to her people and said, 'We shall build our city here, have our children and live in peace.'

"Her mother, who was also her advisor, added, 'And we shall call our city Smyrna, after our beloved Queen, who has fearlessly led us to this paradise on earth.'

"Everyone clapped and cheered. They roasted a small herd of wild goats roaming the hills and had a feast, after sacrificing one on a makeshift altar, to the unknown gods of this foreign land that had now become theirs. It was a wise thing to do, indeed, for the gods had all been watching and they were pleased.

"Keros had her angular face and muscular, sunbathed thighs imprinted on his mind. He was so engrossed in that lingering vision that he got lost on the way to the feast, and arrived late. Considering he was the keeper of time for everyone else, the gods teased him mercilessly the entire night. He chewed at his food mechanically as though it were rubber and barely touched the ambrosia poured into his glass. After a long night of sitting morosely, he turned to Cybele, the goddess of fertility, for sympathy. She was, after all, one who knew about love, however twisted. Every spring she mated with her lover who came to her in the shape of a pig. Then she killed him.

"'What happened on your way here?' Cybele asked him.

"Keros recounted. The feasting gods stopped eating and started listening to his story with great interest. At the end of the story, Keros fell to his knees and begged them to transform him into a man or a woman (in case she was lesbian) or even a horse so she could at least mount him, but they refused to grant his wish. Cybele urged him to get a hold of his senses and move on.

"Poor Keros was sick with love and unable to budge. He forgot about his yodeling friends in the Alps and the pleasure of chasing after time thieves. He spent his days following Smyrna on his cloud everywhere she went, neglecting the rest of the world. And he stopped attending the celestial feasts, despite all the attention bestowed upon him by the gods. Worried about her friend, Cybele went for a visit.

"'My dear Keros, what are you doing to yourself? If you die, the whole universe dies, the Gods die. How can you do this to us? How can you be so besotted with a mere mortal?'

"'I can't help it' he sighed. 'She is why everything matters. She is the one I want to see constantly and when I see others, it is her face I crave. I want children and feasts with her. Hers are the eyes that bring me joy. Do you understand? Hers is the face that brings me pain.'

"'Clearly, you are deranged!' Cybele knew she had to do something if this nonsense was ever to end. 'What happens when she dies?' she asked slyly.

"Her plan was to have Smyrna meet her death accidentally, so Keros would quickly come to grips with her mortality and get back to his celestial business.

"'I will never ever be the keeper of time again. I will retire,' he shrugged.

"Cybele realized the task at hand was more complicated than she initially thought. She ran to the other gods, her dozens of breasts whipping her chest and shoulders, requesting an urgent meeting. That meant a feast had to be prepared, for the Gods never did anything serious without deriving some pleasure from it. At the feast, the gods decided that they would let Keros take the shape of a human briefly, long enough to make her acquaintance and satisfy his longing. Cybele was chosen to bring him the news.

"Days later, as Queen Smyrna went on her usual morning ride along the beach, she curiously noted that the cloud that had been following her for months and months was gone. The ride felt a little lonely without it hovering over her head, as she had grown to enjoy the shade it provided, not to mention the constant company.

"She noticed a tiny rowboat not too far from the rocky shore, with a man in it, his face hidden by a floppy straw hat. She had never seen him there before and decided to slow down to take a good look at him. From far, he had looked like an old man, but as she got closer to him he appeared younger though she could not give him an age. She greeted him and he started rowing towards the shore, to make her acquaintance. After the introduction and a brief exchange of pleasantries, they said goodbye and he rowed back out to the open sea.

"The next day, she found him at the same spot. This went on for a while, and Queen Smyrna started looking forward to these meetings; she perfumed herself with lavender and washed her hair before riding out to meet him, feeling joyful tingling all over her body when the straw hat appeared in the distance. When they sat down on the beach to talk, her cheeks got pinker and her heart fluttered in her chest, like a bird taking flight. Keros was glad he was sitting down, because the human body given to him by the gods did not turn out to be so reliable. He felt his knees shaking and wanting to give in at the sight of her. When he kissed her, he felt a strange sensation which gave his pants a tug. It embarrassed him enormously not to be able to predict what this body was going to do next.

"On their last day, they made love in the shade offered by the rocks on the beach. She did not know this was the last day, and made love to him with all the ardour of her burgeoning passion. He, knowing he would probably never meet her again, loved her with all his exalted and heart-broken desire. They spent the entire day in each other's arms; she, dreaming of the future, and he, trying to forget there was none.

"The next morning Smyrna rode her horse to the place where she always met Keros in his straw hat. There was nobody there. She ran behind the rocks. She ran along the beach calling out his name. She sat down, looked towards the horizon. She started thinking he may have drowned. She waited and waited and at the end of the day, she rode her horse back home. The next day, same thing. And again. Smyrna's daily trips to the rocks became a pilgrimage.

"Keros watched over his lovely Queen from his cloud, feeling that devastated gladness only meant for lovers. He returned with her to the same beach day after day and kept her company from behind his cloud. When she appeared forlorn, he rushed the day along, so it would end faster. On those days when she wandered along the beach whistling a little tune and talking to him out loud, he let the day last as long as he could allow it.

"Meanwhile her belly started rising, and her breast filled with life. No one knew who the father was and she never told, for she was the Queen and accountable to no human. Her little boy eventually also had dreams in which he played with a man in a straw hat. When he told his mother about them, she smiled.

"'That is your father' she explained, 'he will visit you every night.'

"Thus, the love affair continued through the years, as mother and son rode their horses along the beach followed by a cloud.

"Smyrna grew old and withered in time, as humans inevitably do, and finally died. Keros, devastated, dragged himself on and away. He was gone for a very long while and the gods, in his absence, scrambled to do his job. He did return eventually, for his child needed guidance, and then his grandchildren, and great-grandchildren. Thus it is said that Keros still hovers over Smyrna on a white fluffy cloud, to watch over his descendants. You rarely see a cloud in the sky, but when you do, you know it belongs to him. And when it rains in June for just one day, as it always does, you know Keros is weeping for his lost Smyrna. And so," Polycarp concluded with a sigh, "this is why time weighs upon the soul in Smyrna and its passing fills the heart with grief."

Niko listened, transfixed. Whenever he had a question, his uncle made sure the answer was never brief or dismissive. It was mostly for his own enjoyment, for he loved to see that young face with wide open eyes, and mouth ajar, feet dangling from the chair that was still a bit high for his legs, listening with delight. He never told the same story twice, because he invented them all on the spot and forgot about them as soon as they left his lips.

A Gondolier in Venice

THAT VERY SAME AFTERNOON as Niko sat listening to the story of Smyrna up in Polycarp's room, a young Greek doctor moved to Aya Katerina. The neighbourhood was abuzz with gossip when the carriages arrived with his boxes and furniture. Some ooh'ed that he did not have a wife and took their unmarried daughters for a quick walk by his house, others aah'ed because he came from Thessaloniki and was the son of a rich landowner. His name was Manolis. He had impeccable clothes and manners, züppe,* according to Polycarp, who never warmed up to him. His parents were landowners from Focia, the town with windmills on the Aegean coast, north of Smyrna. They were well-off, he had studied to be a doctor in Constantinople and had lived in Thessaloniki for some years. His grandmother's house had been next door to Marie's, when Jacob, Elena and Polycarp were children. Manolis used to spend the summer at his grandmother's house and they were all childhood friends. He called Marie "Thia," aunt.

The house was boarded up and it remained uninhabited except for the occasional visit from a gardener or a housekeeper who made sure everything was in order. A week before his arrival, the gardener and the housekeeper had worked in the house together, bringing along painters and carpenters. Everyone knew changes were afoot.

*a dandy

After inspecting the area quickly, Manolis hurried to Marie's house to see his old friends. Niko, hearing the commotion from Polycarp's room upstairs, went to the window and saw the young man climb their front steps with a bouncy hop and knock on the door. His shiny black hair was combed back. His fashionable moustache, which curled up on the sides, was accompanied by long sideburns. The cream-coloured suit was perfectly pressed.

When Elena opened the door, he exclaimed, "Elena?"

She nodded yes, and just as she was about to rejoin "And you are . . . ?" he picked her up and whirled her around like a dervish before putting her down.

"Don't you remember me?" he exclaimed as she took a moment to adjust.

Her face slowly lit up into a smile. "Manolis!"

She remembered indeed, blushing slightly as she said, "You've changed! Where are those dirty knobby knees full of scabs?"

He laughed, hugging her again.

"I still remember those beatings you gave me. I doubt you could do that now," he said and straightened his chest.

"Hey, don't push your luck!"

They entered the house arm in arm.

"Mama, Pol, come see who's here!" she shouted before realizing that they were all there already, waiting for their turn to hug him.

By the time they sat down for coffee, Manolis had lost his smile because they had told him about Jacob. To lighten his mood, Marie asked him about his move to Smyrna. He explained that he had always wanted to live here. Ever since he started spending the summers at his grandmother's, he had felt the pull. And anyway, he wasn't from Greece and did not feel at home there, he was Anatolian, this was his home. He had to decide between Focia, Constantinople, and Smyrna, and felt Smyrna was the best choice for him, due to the great number of Greeks living here and the pleasant city life.

Marie noticed that as he spoke he stole a few glances in Elena's direction. Since childhood, Manolis had had a secret crush on Elena. She had been too busy playing and fighting with the boys in the neighbourhood to notice anything. He often let her win so she would feel stronger. In fact, all the boys in the neighbourhood were infatuated with her and competed for her attention. She was muscular and headstrong, could run as fast as a boy and never cried when she got hurt. When she had the measles and was in bed for almost the entire summer, the boys did not play "çelik çomak." This was a game played with a stick and a can of soup and vaguely resembled baseball or cricket. It was her favourite game and no one played it until she was well enough to run around again.

That summer of her sickness she had tossed a penny from her window, while talking with Manolis, who was on the street. He took the penny and hid it in his grandmother's backyard, in a hole that he dug and covered up again. Like a pirate with his hidden treasure of gold, he would check the hole every few days to make sure the penny was still there.

Manolis felt again the heave in his chest return from that childhood crush as they talked about the old days.

Marie asked, "So, do you have a fiancée yet?"

He had had one. She was in Greece. She did not see herself living in Smyrna, so they broke off. An awkard silence followed, after which Manolis addressed Niko,

"Would you like to see a camera?"

Niko shook his head yes.

"It is somewhere in those boxes." Manolis waved a hand towards his house. "Once I dig it up, I'll bring it over so you can learn to take pictures. And now I must go and help the men."

He rose and gave Marie another hug before leaving. They all sat breathing his lingering scent with a smile, except for Polycarp, who remained unimpressed.

"Do you believe the fiancée left him because she didn't want to come here?"

All eyes turned to him and he shrugged. "He probably dressed better than she did. She got bored waiting for him to curl his moustache before leaving the house."

Elena threw a cushion at him and burst into laughter. Marie rose to go back to the kitchen, protesting, "Don't destroy my cushions, you barbarians!"

And thus Manolis began his new life in Smyrna, having biscuit and tea in the afternoons in Marie's backyard, playing tavla* with Polycarp while ogling Elena as she painted bowls of fruits that looked like genitals. Whenever he came for a visit, he left a note on his door in case of a medical emergency, and brought along his brown leather bag and his dog Katzathoro, who spread himself on the cool stones.

Polycarp, when he saw them coming, would exclaim, "You're itching for humiliation again? Don't you have any patients left? Have you killed them all?" To which Manolis would smile, shake his head and reply, "Let's see who's going to humiliate whom this time . . ."

Polycarp would frown and point at the dog. "You've brought your snoring carpet too."

It seemed no Polycarpian insult deterred Manolis and his phlegmatic companion from visiting. Marie was the only one whose delight was flagrant. She brought out trays of Turkish coffee, called him Manolaki, and even pulled the tips of his perfectly groomed black moustache and smacked him on the back of the head to show her affection.

"Eat, eat. Why aren't you eating? You don't like it?"

His tavla-playing afternoons were often interrupted by emergency calls. A boy of about eight would come knocking, to fetch him. Pol would close the tavla set a little too fast and shout, "Time to kill some patients!"

After he left, one day, Pol complained to his mother, "I don't like

*backgammon

this constant tavla-playing with the züppe! Why must you feed and cajole him so? I need some peace and quiet, don't you understand?"

Marie frowned and hissed, pointing her chin at her daughter, "Look at the strange things she's painting . . . You want her to become crazy like you? She needs to get married, have children, do real things, put away those smelly brushes."

Elena became furious. She screamed, broke a few things, slammed doors, and refused to eat for a few days. Her mother brought her bowls of soup and cups of tea in order to be forgiven. She knocked on the door and pleaded. Elena simply told her to go away. When she finally emerged from her room, looking gaunt and faded, Marie was so shocked that she never spoke ill of her paintings again. Manolis, however, continued to visit.

Niko, like his grandmother, enjoyed Manolis's presence. He was allowed to play with the stethoscope and touch the camera that Manolis occasionally brought over with considerable pomp. He would mount it on a tripod, hide under the black curtain and take pictures. He never failed to recount the story of how he got it in Constantinople.

Dr Karalis, a gynecologist and professor of his, happened to be a camera collector. During a very difficult breach delivery, he jokingly promised a camera to his student—the brightest of them all, needless to say—Manolis if he managed to deliver the infant safely without help. During the operation it became apparent that there was yet another baby. Manolis, as he recounted the story, was practically drowning in blood, sweat, and amniotic fluid when he realized, after having safely gotten the first one out, that the second one was also a breach. Dr Karalis decided to take over, reassuring his student that he had already deserved his camera. But the brilliant and able Manolis managed to deliver the second one too. And this was how the Camera of the Breach Twins came to Smyrna to take so many pictures.

Polycarp was skeptical as usual. He shrugged, not even looking up from his bowl of half-peeled green peas, and offered, "Why don't you just tell the child the truth? You stole it from a patient too sick to object. And it's called The Camera of the Dead Patient."

Elena looked at Polycarp from her still life that looked positively lifeless—a vase of wilted flowers next to a limp, plucked, and beheaded rooster—and smiled. Manolis, heartened by the smile (even though it wasn't for him), approached her easel and after a polite inspection, nodded. "Very pretty. Yes . . . Why not also paint something more . . . Like Venice! Imagine a canal at sunset. Lovers in a gondola. An accordion-player somewhere, playing his sad music. Would make a nice picture . . . " His hands, making air drawings of gondolas and accordions, came to a full stop as he bent his head to one side with a disarming smile.

Elena was about to say something sharp. Instead, she smiled again and replied, "I'll paint you a Venice if you like. You can hang it in your clinic."

Manolis blushed with pleasure.

It took weeks and was a tortured affair. She started it over and over. She threw her brushes down in frustration. Capricious Venice would not allow herself to be painted. Instead of dropping the idea, which everybody encouraged her to do, Elena became obsessed with gondolas. She went to Mr Clementini's bookstore and asked for a book on Venice. He had none. She went to another bookseller on Fasula. He had none either, but unwilling to lose a customer, ran his fingers through his imaginary hair (he was bald), lifted his thick glasses over the bridge of his aquiline nose and said, "I think I have something . . . "

He disappeared into the back of the store and returned a short while later with a dusty postcard. Someone, the rich lady for whom his sister Louise, who was a seamstress, sewed clothes, had spent her honeymoon in Venice—before the war, of course. What a coincidence, ha ha ha . . . Now if you don't mind the writing on the back, you can have it. No no, no need to pay anything. It's just an old postcard.

Elena returned home and immediately sat down to paint. The

accordion-player played alone on a gondola, at sunset. The dark canal seemed endlessly long and ominous, flanked by houses that were sinking into the depths like ships. The musician, oblivious to the dangers lurking ahead, played with his eyes closed and his head tilted. He had a melancholy smile on his face as his gondola drifted on.

When Elena presented Manolis with her version of Venice, he took one brief and somewhat baffled look, thanked her, embraced the canvas and carried it clumsily to his house with funereal dignity.

Elena looked at him from the living room window until he disappeared from view.

"Are you sad because he didn't like your painting?" Niko asked.

She looked surprised, as though she hadn't considered the possibility at all.

"You think he didn't?" She continued gazing at the empty street with blank eyes.

"I think he expected something different. More like . . . "

The boy started searching for a way to end the sentence, which evaporated as Elena stared with eyebrows raised.

" . . . the pictures in Three-Fingered Adem's butcher shop, for example," he finished lamely just as she was turning away.

"You mean he wanted cows swimming in Venetian canals?" She giggled.

It wounded his pride. He took on a more decisive tone. "He wanted something that people expect to see."

"What is that, then?" She looked serious.

"Well, when you look at the pictures in Three-Fingered Adem's store, cows and sheep graze in pastures. The sun is shining. Nobody's getting slaughtered. It's just something to look at while you wait."

She nodded as though she understood.

Three-Fingered Adem

THAT AFTERNOON SHE TOOK her nephew by the arm and out they went, marching at her usual hurried pace towards Fasula. Niko was annoyed not knowing where he was being taken or why, besides which he had a game of marbles planned with friends. Objections did not appear to matter to his aunt, who steered through the streets dragging the boy along. Entering Fasula, she slowed down, allowing him to take in the scene. A woman in rags, leaning on a wall, eyes closed, begging in a faint sing-song voice, her three small children clutching at her skirts. The fragrance of roasted coffee wafting over the citrus stalls, mixing with the smell of sweetmeats and blood from butcher shops. Fish heads on sidewalks, half-eaten by cats. The freshly baked frangiolas lining the bakery window. The jeweller sitting on a stool by his shop, flashing a golden eyetooth at Elena approvingly. His sausage-shaped pinkie had an enormous ring glittering around it. He had stretched it out like a fat ballerina about to do a pirouette, while his index finger and thumb nonchalantly released the worry beads one on top of the other with the precision of water dropping from a leaking tap. They passed the stall selling spices and herbs of all shades of brown and green in large bags made of hemp. The bags smelled of shipwrecks and pirates, of brown-skinned women with long necks, and strange goats on mountaintops carrying little men with big hats. The linden leaves smelled of nostalgia, like his mother whom he could smell no more.

"Here," said his aunt abruptly as she stopped in front of Adem's butcher shop named Fotini, after his Greek wife. They were Cretan.

After the Greek and Turkish greetings, Elena said, "Niko here is fond of your store. He likes the pictures." Her hand waved carelessly all around.

Adem smiled and nodded his head.

"Tea?" he offered.

"Thanks, we just had some."

He nodded again with a courteous smile, waiting for the order.

Elena smiled apologetically. "Adem Bey, I am not here to buy anything today. I would like to make a painting of your shop for him, since he likes it so. Would you mind sitting in that chair below the painting for a few minutes while I sketch?"

Adem Bey looked out the window. There was no one coming towards the store. He obliged, with shy pride, quickly combing his hair back with his fingers. His helper stopped splitting bones and slicing livers, and Elena's hands flew across her sketching paper. Of her three sketches, she offered the best to Adem Bey as a souvenir. After goodbyes in Greek and Turkish, away they went, leaving Adem Bey and his assistant to contemplate the sketch.

The oil portrait of Three-Fingered Adem took her one month to complete. Niko was not allowed to look at it until she called him into her room one morning before he went off to school. She had the painting draped with a sheet. He pulled it down to find himself face to face with Kasap Adem sitting gingerly on a faded wicker chair, in front of his picture of grazing cows, surrounded by heavy carcasses and body parts hanging on brass hooks, his apron stained with blood. His hands were crossed on his lap, the three fingers on the left hand holding on to the other five like drowning children. His red moustache rested proudly on his good-natured lips. In one corner Elena had written, "To Niko, with love." At the back of the canvas, she had put in careful oil brush, "Kasap Adem in his shop,

Smyrna 1919."

Niko asked her to hang it in his room, across from his bed. Every morning when he woke up, Kasap Adem greeted him, and every night as he was doing homework, he absentmindedly observed the painting. He daydreamed over math problems, looking at the hanging legs of lamb or focused on the bloodstained apron while trying to memorize Lafontaine's fables. He gazed at the nervous brushstrokes and the way the oil paint caked up in parts, looking grotesque from up close. As he slowly moved away, the painting came into focus. He tried to understand how this could happen; how a globby brushstroke that left an untidy trail behind could make a man's mouth come alive. Was it a lucky coincidence? When he watched her, she painted up close, then moved back a bit, then reached closer to place a brushstroke, then back again and forth to smear paint with a cloth or a spatula, then back out again like a docile boxer slowed down by the years. Some days she sat in the attic gazing blankly at a canvas for hours. Trying to understand how his aunt painted seemed a greater challenge to him than his studies; and a far more satisfying preoccupation. He had run his fingers over the surface of the painting, feeling the bumps and grooves left by her brush so frequently that he knew its entire texture by heart, and he could dream of it as an enormous surface on which he, a tiny insect, climbed and advanced for what seemed like hours and hours, first on a scarlet terrain, up and down the mounds, then through various other shades, searching for a green oasis. On the days when he felt blue, the three remaining fingers of Adem's left hand made him weep for his lost parents.

How to Swallow a Fly

SCHOOL WAS COLLÈGE ST JOSEPH, run by French Catholic friars, wrapped in black robes and white beards, with looks of stern purpose and armed with pointers to point at the board. Niko enjoyed the tick-tick made every time Frère Felix showed Abyssinia or the Amazon River or something else on the world map. What he enjoyed most was being sent out of the classroom as punishment, to stand in the corridor until the end of the class. The corridor was lined with wooden shelves protected by locked glass doors. On the shelves were stuffed birds—a couple of dusty bald eagles, an owl, a flamingo, a crane, pickled amphibians in various stages of growth in big jars, and a human male fetus with the umbilical cord still attached, floating in liquid, its eyes closed. Even though he was expected to stand in a corner, his fascination made him go back and forth in the corridor. Once in a while the friar would stick his head out of the classroom to find him observing the jars at the other end of the corridor.

"Devision, mais que vous ai-je dit?" his voice would boom, and the boy would come running back to his corner. "Je m'excuse cher Frère," he would mumble only to wander off a few minutes later.

Frère Felix had affectionately nicknamed Niko "le paillaçon," the clown. The boy had a talent for making the class laugh. Even Frère Felix, who was the grimmest teacher in the school, had to turn his back to the class with a frown, to secretly smile under his thick moustache at Niko's clownish acts. He was tiresome and disruptive but got top marks in all the subjects. Frère Felix grudgingly admired this effervescent young mind, who was the brightest he had taught in his long career.

During recess, on rainy days, Niko amused his classmates by drawing on the chalkboard. He would start from an unlikely point of departure, and the boys would bet their precious money on the finished subject. Those who bet on a nude woman might find instead a braying donkey staring at them.

Once, during a long and boring account of the Napoleonic wars, Niko went hopping up and down in his seat pretending to catch flies and stuff them in his mouth, chewing them with convincing relish. Frère Felix progressively turning red at the giggling and squirming waited until Niko actually caught a fly in his fist to suddenly interrupt his lecture.

"Mangez-la!" he ordered.

Niko grew pale, feeling the ticklish buzz of the fly's wings in his closed fist.

"Allez, avalez-la, je vous dis!" Frère Felix thundered.

"Mais, cher Frère, je vous demande pardon, je ne le ferais plus," implored the boy.

"D'abord, vous mangerez votre mouche," replied the friar, his bushy eyebrows knit into one unyielding mass.

Thus, Niko ate his fly. He ran out of the classroom to vomit, and that same day he was suspended from school.

His grandmother, who had seen him come home from school suspended once too often, marched him to her brother Constantine, who was busy cleaning his tavern before the afternoon rush. Constantine took out his belt from around his enormous girth and threatened to whip the boy's bare legs, but as usual did not do so. Instead, he dragged the boy down the stairs by one firmly grasped ear and locked him up in the wine cellar. It was dark in there and tomb-like. Niko imagined gutter rats creeping past his feet every time he heard a rustle or a creak. He dared not sit from fear of being bitten. The darkness was so absolute that his eyes never adjusted to it. He started sobbing, begging his great-uncle for mercy as loud as his lungs could afford.

Constantine, who had never had children of his own, could not stand the screaming and sobbing for too long. He unlocked the cellar door and motioned for the child to come upstairs. By the same ear he pulled him and sat him on a bar stool. "Listen well, Nicolas, if you do not wish to be stuck in that cellar again—and I promise you next time, I will leave you there the entire day—you better quit acting like a clown at school. Your grandmother has much to worry about already. You understand?"

Niko nodded yes, sniffling and rubbing his ear.

"Run along then and no more suspensions from school, you hear? Or else . . . " threatened the fat great-uncle, wiping the sweat trickling down his neck with a folded handkerchief, his eyes crowned by a terrorizing frown.

Later, Niko did not remember the date or year of this incident. He simply recalled it was a Wednesday. He returned home, having occasional spasms of repulsion on the way, recalling the feel of the fly in his mouth and his uncle's frightening cellar. He walked straight up to his room and closed his door without speaking to anyone. Hiding under the bed covers he whispered repeatedly, "Mama. I feel so alone."

That Wednesday, as always, Ayşe Hanım came by with her sack of dandelions, and Marie sat her on a chair and made her tea. Ayşe Hanım was a diminutive lady bent half at the waist. She had luminously blue Circassian eyes and thick uncombed grey hair bunched together under a kerchief. She wore the same shalvar* always, with patches covering the holes. When she opened her mouth, the

*baggy pants

wounded seats of her absent front teeth appeared raw and deep. Her nose and the right side of her face were gnarled like an olive tree. When she smiled, which was quite rare, it chilled Niko's blood.

Radhikya* grew on her mountains. She brought a couple of kilos at a time for Marie and a few neighbours. This was her livelihood, and they suspected she had no home but lived among dandelions and trees. As Marie washed the radhikya leaves in the kitchen, Ayşe would lament, rocking herself back and forth. "Ah my ruthless fate, merciful Allah, why did you not kill me?"

Her two sons had fought in the Balkans. One died. They brought back the other on a stretcher with stumps for legs and a bullet in his head. He didn't recognize her. He didn't remember his own name. She hit her head on a rock, to die, such was her sorrow, but she only managed to break her face. Kismet. Allah gives, Allah takes away.

Ayşe's frail body reminded one of a dying sparrow, huddled and trembling from head to toe, its eyes closed, finding no solace in the warm sun or the rustle of leaves, oblivious to the indolent crawl of an earthworm nearby. Merely breathing, waiting to die. Polycarp stayed in his room every Wednesday. He hid under his bed and put a pillow over his head. Niko never figured out whether he did it to block out her lamenting or his own, but he used to hear them both.

That day, after Ayşe left, Polycarp went down to the kitchen and grabbed the old green chair Marie used to climb to reach for the jars in the pantry. He took it out to the yard, fetched the axe and under his mother's horrified gaze broke it.

They all thought he'd gone mad again. Marie kept urging Niko to go fetch Manolis, but he couldn't keep his eyes off Polycarp. His pyjamas blew around his emaciated body like a striped flag on a pole. He got out nails, a saw, a hammer, and started working. Not once did he look up. Marie wiped her hands on her apron and dropped into a chair. Slowly she understood that he was making a pair of crutches. They were quite stubby when finished, almost

*dandelions

like toys, but Ayşe's son did not need tall ones anyway, having no legs at all.

Later, upon his request, Marie sewed two cushions for the boy's armpits. Polycarp wrapped the crutches and cushions in an old newspaper and left them on the kitchen table for Ayşe to take home the next time she came. He never spent another Wednesday in the house.

Niko, in whose memory this Wednesday remained engraved for life, took out a notebook from his school bag and started writing the first of his two thousand lines in his best calligraphy, "I will not disrupt the class." After line number five, he counted the number of lines on one page, and figured he had to write about thirty-six more pages. He wondered if he could count a skipped line as one. He wrote one more line and was exhausted.

A Hat Worth Three Kurush

WHEN HE WAS NOT SITTING at home in his pyjamas, Polycarp went to Jacob's hat store to mind it. At times Elena and Marie joined him. Jacob made ladies' hats mostly, and occasionally gentlemans' bowlers. The narrow store had a long counter on which mannequin heads were lined up wearing colourful hats. Elena had painted faces on them so that they looked like Marie-Antoinette and her ladies, bald and beheaded, yet smiling elegantly. When the women came, the little bells at the door ringing furiously, Polycarp would sigh and whisper, "Here come the cows."

Often the place was so dusty that Niko could write his name on the shelves with his finger. Sometimes one of the women came to clean the shop. Polycarp could not be bothered. He preferred to sit behind the counter reading his books, resenting every interruption. He did not even attempt to hide his displeasure when the customers came, and gradually their number decreased. It was suggested that it would be best if Elena minded the store. "She smiles and it's easier to speak with her."

At the back were the presses, irons, and machines used to give a hat its form. There were stacks of fabric in different colors and textures. When Marie or Elena were minding the front, Polycarp worked in the back. Ladies came in, chose a model from a catalogue or from one of the mannequin heads. Then the rolls of fabric came out for selection. A week later the customer returned to try her hat on for modifications, and the hat was finished in a couple more days. But sometimes it wasn't. Polycarp, who did not have much patience for manual tasks, would have cut the fabric a little too close and had to start all over again with a brand new hat.

One day Madame Vidory walked in like a well-fed turkey, announced by a vigourous chime of bells, and demanded her hat, impatiently tapping her red fingertips on the glass showcase.

"Monsieur Devision!"

Tap tap tap. She was wearing a feathered hat, which only emphasized her ornithological qualities.

"Mais . . . Etes-vous là?" she huffed.

Her head stretched back and forth as she showed her extreme annoyance at not being served immediately. When Polycarp parted the curtain at the back to show his face, she exclaimed, "Ah le voilà! Vous, Monsieur, vous n'êtes pas Jacob, c'est sûr."

Polycarp retorted, "Et vous, Madame, vous n'êtes certainement pas la reine d'Angleterre."

"Ma cappeline, s'il vous plaît!" she threw back with disdain, looking out the window to emphasize her displeasure at seeing him. Polycarp went to the back of the store, to fetch her hat, muttering "Grosse vache" under his breath.

"Pardon?" she responded haughtily still looking out the window.

"Je disais que j'ai une grosse tache . . . " He rubbed the sleeve of his shirt.

When he looked on the shelf for the woman's wide-brimmed hat, it was not there. Instead, he found one in red velvet, with a tiny upturned border on one side and a bow on the other. Her name was written on a piece of paper under it. He remembered. He sighed and pulled the curtain aside to face Madame Vidory, holding it in his hand.

"Mais, ce n'est pas mon chapeau! Je vous avais commandé une cappeline," she stressed the last word in alarm.

"Madame Vidory," he sighed, "forgive me, but . . . why would you want to wear a cappeline, when it went out of fashion twenty years ago? Small hats are all the rage now. I simply refuse to let a good customer like you wear an enormous unflattering red hat, like some Porthos in a skirt."

He stopped and took a breath, measuring the effect of the last sentence, before he added,

"Unless it was for a costume ball?"

Madame Vidory's blood pressure had very evidently risen, from the look of her red cheeks. Polycarp continued,

"If you're not pleased with this, I can always make the hat you had asked for, free of charge. Just give me a couple of days. But why don't you try it on, at least."

Looking somewhat confused, she hesitated between leaving the shop and trying on the new hat. She looked towards the street and then back at the hat. It did look rather charming and dainty. Polycarp's comment about her resembling a fat musketeer had deflated her outrage, replacing it with the fear of ridicule.

"But Monsieur," she uttered plaintively, "why did you not give me the choice when I came in the first time?"

He nodded, "I should have. And I apologize, Madame." With an air of pained resolve he added, "You can pick up your cappeline in a couple of days. Madame Misich was in yesterday. I showed it to her for style. She was begging to buy it. I refused to let her try it on. I think she will be pleased to have it, now."

Madame Misich was Madame Vidory's arch-enemy. They were neighbours, and only a week ago due to a septic tank problem involving their adjacent properties, they had exchanged scatological insults loudly in the church courtyard after Sunday mass. Polycarp knew he had sold the hat.

"Ah, non! Pas elle . . . " She grabbed the hat. "Combien?" she asked, opening her purse.

Polycarp could never say "three" without stuttering. The number was painful, he had to avoid all conversations that required its utterance. His hand went to his left ear and he twisted it lightly, a gesture he made whenever "three" required mentioning. He hesitated, clearing his throat.

"Thh . . . Four!"

"What do you mean?" She frowned.

"The price. It costs four kurush."

"That's not what you said last week. You said three."

"I could not have said that."

"You did too!"

"It wasn't me."

"It was your sister, then. Still, it was three."

"I will not argue for one kurush, Madame Vidory. Take it."

He impatiently wrapped the hat and gave it to her. Madame Vidory left the store feeling quite pleased with herself on three accounts: she had avoided ridicule, saved one kurush, and won an imaginary hat war against the despicable Madame Misich. On the sidewalk, she swayed left and right as she walked until she stepped on a loose tile, releasing a spray of water. Niko, who was observing her from the window, saw her cursing and wiping her calves, bent over like a washerwoman, momentarily relinquishing the ladylike demeanour she tried so hard to project as a wealthy Levantine.

Thus, due to Polycarp's accident with the scissors, wide-brimmed hats went completely out of fashion in Smyrna in a relatively short time. Instead, all the women in the vicinity wore variations of the same bucket-like hat that looked like a cross between a fez and a bowler with flowers or bows on the side.

The store had belonged to their father, Jacob, who, in his youth, had put all his life savings into buying it and the house. In Jacob's absence the store was not a money-maker. Although Polycarp modified fashion to compensate for his difficulty with the scissors, not everyone was as easily swayed as Mme Vidory. Some ladies demanded the hats be redone. Polycarp's stuttering with the number "three" did not always translate to a sale of four kurush; occasionally the hat went for two.

Marie was glad the store was there to give her children a reason to get up and go someplace every morning. She hoped the routine would help change Polycarp's morose inclinations and odd behaviour. She started pushing Elena to join her brother, hoping her daughter would divert her obsession with painting towards a more practical occupation. What this accomplished, however, was quite different. Elena carried her easel to the shop, where she continued painting in the back room, while Polycarp brought his books and started placing them side by side on shelves where hats used to rest. They stayed in the shop late into the evening, enjoying the quietude it offered.

Frenk Sokağı was a busy street. The mornings started with the squeaky sounds of metal shutters rolling up, and voices rising in the early sunlight, accompanied by the smell of tea brewing in the teahouse. The tea boy poked his head into the store at exactly eight every morning, "çay?" and came swinging his tray filled with the tea glasses on their saucers, tiny spoons for the two sugar cubes on the side. Every time the door swung open, the festive little bells chimed, letting in the algae and iodine smell of the sea with bits of conversations, laughter, the occasional meow of a stray cat, and the clip-clopping of a horse.

Niko started going to the shop straight from school, and did his homework sitting by his uncle behind the counter. The customers enjoyed the young boy's presence, his smile and wide-open eyes when he listened to them. Since he had no problem uttering "three kurush," everyone paid the correct price for their hats when he was around. He enjoyed spending time in the shop because it reminded him of his father. When there were no customers around, he went to the back, sniffing and smelling objects, half expecting to encounter him there.

He had been told many times by his grandmother how his father and mother had worked in the store together, two lovebirds stealing kisses and exchanging meaningful glances that escaped no one. This story, which was meant to appease his tormented soul, saddened him even more, since he felt responsible for seperating them by coming into the world. His father had refused to get remarried, despite everyone's advice. Widowers rarely remained unmarried in those days. There was always a woman whom her family was eager to "place." Niko absentmindedly stroked the back of his father's old armchair before sitting in it. Why did I have the parents I had and not others? Why do I live in this family and not in another?

Polycarp looked up from his books vaguely and responded, "You're right, of course."

Niko ignored his uncle, who went on, "And why are you yourself and not somebody else? It logically follows to ask this question, doesn't it?"

"You can't not ask the questions," he went on, as if prompted to delve deeper. "Doesn't mean there is an answer. Actually, it's better not to get answers to some . . . See, it works like this: questions are space-openers in the mind, answers are doors you can close. If all the doors are closed, you end up in a perfect square. How interesting is that? And anyway, just because you closed a door doesn't mean the question has gone away, you've simply chosen to leave it outside. Some people can go through life inside a perfect square. Others pretend they can, until the piles and piles of questions crammed at the doorstep find a way to seep in, and then it gets pretty messy. They go crazy, jump out windows, etc . . . "

"Is that what happened to you?" asked Niko.

"No, my boy . . . I'm unable even to recognize the doors," Polycarp smiled weakly. "I have this recurrent nightmare of floating in space alone. There is nothing familiar, even my body appears unattached."

At that moment, Marie walked in noisily, and put down a big basket, having evidently strained herself.

"I waited and waited, reheated supper twice but you never showed up!" she said in a tone of exasperation.

Niko looked out the window. The street was dark and deserted.

"I brought it here." She took out cutlery and plates.

They pushed aside the heads of Marie Antoinette lookalikes and set the table on the counter. The bean stew was still hot, with a spoonful of fresh creamy yogurt beside it. They hadn't seen yoghurt in months. There was no bread, Marie explained. She did not have the strength to line up for it. Niko loved this side of his grandmother. She did everything matter-of-factly. If her kids didn't show up for supper; she showed up with it. Even when she was grumpy, he was assured of her unwavering devotion. They ate absentmindedly. Niko chewed, thinking of his uncle floating in space. The image made him shudder; to be so lost was frightening. Marie stared at Elena's forehead, which had a slash of blue paint across it. Elena was oblivious. Polycarp mused about his nephew's loneliness and how to remedy it. Thus they finished the bean stew and yogurt. Polycarp rose, rubbing his stomach. "We may be the first humans to go to the moon, tonight," he said. Niko added. "We should hold hands, so no one gets lost in space."

They picked up the dirty plates and cutlery, placed them in the basket after rinsing them in the backroom, and walked home, holding hands under the quiet watch of the full moon and the flickering gas lights of the streets. Halfway to the house, Polycarp exclaimed, "Oh no . . . Oh no . . . Niko hold my hand tight, I think we're going to the moon!" He let out a trumpeting fart into the night. When later he got into bed, Niko was still giggling.

Mount Pagus

CONSTANTINE, MARIE'S YOUNGER BROTHER, owned a tavern in Pasaport, where the ships docked and passed customs. The Austrian post office was nearby. The Ottoman one, although a little farther out, was close enough for its tired employees to come and have a drink at the end of the day. Constantine's wine seemed to please everyone equally. He spoke at least five languages fluently and got by in a few more. It was not unusual for someone from Smyrna to be a polyglot, since each family could trace several ethnic backgrounds in its makeup. Everyone spoke Turkish and Greek and, depending on the family background, also a selection from German, English, French, and Italian. French was somewhat common among all the middle classes, considered to be the language of the educated and refined. Uncle Constantine was able to speak to everyone, which may have been the reason for his tavern's success. It was always packed full in the evenings, even as the war raged on. Despite all other shortages, he seemed to have an endless supply of wine, for which he charged a different price each day.

Due to his financial ease, he was able to help Marie and her family, buying them their occasional pairs of shoes, school supplies for Niko, and luxuries such as butter and milk that were hard to find. He gave his sister an allowance, knowing that the hat business was not exactly thriving. Marie found it hard to receive charity, even from her own brother. She often sent Elena and Niko to help out at the tavern in the evenings, as repayment. Elena helped in the kitchen while Niko swept floors and filled glasses of wine. He dreaded the thought of being sent to the cellar to get things, and would busy himself away from his great-uncle's sight.

Constantine's wife Carmela would be frying sardines and preparing mézé to go with the wine and raki. She never passed unnoticed. Her abundant behind rebelliously followed her body, shaking like two mountains caught in an earthquake. Her breasts, affectionately called "Les Balcons," were like the Twin Mountains of Izmir.* You could see them from any angle, even from behind. Her striking immensity was a beautiful thing to watch. Having no children of her own, she showed much affection towards Niko, squeezing him into her soft, warm bosom and caressing his hair while the boy tried to get a closer look at her fleshy balconies.

American and British marines, Greeks, Italians, and Turks were all talking at once, laughing, smoking, and drinking. An American and a British sailor came to blows, got a few bruises, then shook hands and continued drinking. Later, an Italian sailor patted Aunt Carmela's bottom while she was passing by with a tray of mézés. He said he couldn't help himself, "Ché culo splendido, madonna mia!" and proceeded to cross himself.

Constantine threw him out, and scolded his wife for causing a disruption with her rear. Elena shoved a tray of sardines into Niko's hands, sending him out of the kitchen as the couple's voices rose above the sizzle of sardines and the buzz of conversations in the tavern. Constantine, it seemed, focused all his misfortunes on his wife's bottom when he felt unhappy. Having no children was due to her bottom, and so were fights in the tavern and the damage done by drunks. Whenever they had a dispute, it started with her bottom and spiraled down to his not having studied architecture in his youth, which of course he also blamed on her fleshy extension.

Sami Bey winked at Niko, saying to Elena, "We better forget

*Smyrna

about having more sardines tonight. They'll be too toasty."

He took out his pocket watch.

"In fifteen minutes, I bet one kurush Constantine will open that door, and say, 'Sorry folks, no more sardines. Have a drink on the house.' You know, they'd save a lot of money if they stopped fighting like this . . . "

Kiryo Costa, Sami Bey's drinking buddy, bet two kurush Constantine would take seventeen minutes. Others in the tavern joined the bet. Pocket watches were placed on the table and they all started waiting, eyes fixed on the kitchen door.

Elena, offended by the scene, moved away and sat at an empty table with her drawing pad, looking around for a subject to sketch. There was a young foreigner in his early twenties, sitting alone by a window, occasionally writing on a pad of paper before placing his pen between his nose and mouth, daydreaming. He smoked a pipe, too. He resembled Jacob in his youth. The same square jaw, same wise, melancholy gaze. Elena asked for his order, her heart beating wildly even though her mind kept insisting this could not be Jacob; he was dead. Nothing but a coincidence. She cleared her throat and asked in Turkish if he was ready to order. The man looked up, shaking his head with a smile, "Didn't understand a word you said."

"Ah . . . You English?"

"No. American."

"Drink?"

"Scotch."

"No."

She shook her head pointing at the barrels to make him understand. "Vin. Vino. Krasi. Yes. Scotch, no. Raki yes."

"Raki, yes." He smiled. Then moving his hand towards his mouth, he asked, "Mangiare?"

She nodded no, and looked towards the kitchen door, which was still closed. "In a little while."

She decided Italian was the language to speak with the American. "Fried sardines on the menu today; I can bring you some in about twenty minutes with bean salad and bread."

"Grazie."

Elena smiled, putting her small writing pad in her apron. He noticed her hands were trembling.

At the bar, Niko approached her. "Did you notice?"

She nodded and looked away to hide her trembling chin.

"He looks exactly like Papa," mused Niko. "Is he a ghost?"

Elena caressed the boy's head. "I haven't pinched him, yet. Shall I?"

He continued staring as Elena brought the American his raki. The kitchen door swung open at the same time, and as predicted by Sami Bey, the drinks were on the house. There was a round of applause and laughter. It appeared Kiryo Kostas had won the bet this time. He gathered the money and declared that the next round was on him. Elena told the American he was lucky. He wouldn't have to pay for this drink, or the next one.

"Are Ottomans always so generous?" asked the American, amused.

"Long story . . . " She shrugged.

"Would you sit with me?" he asked.

"No, thanks," she smiled, businesslike.

"I'd like to hear the long story."

"Here, women don't drink with strangers, unless they are . . . you know . . . " she said firmly.

"Where I come from, women do as they please. Not just if they are . . . you know . . . "

"Really?" asked Elena.

"Uh-uh . . . "

"They can vote too, can't they?"

"I think so."

Elena hesitated for a moment then said, "Perhaps just one drink."

She went to get herself a glass of raki. She swung her hips a little. Heads turned and everyone gaped as she sat with the American and lifted her glass.

"My name is Hemingway," he smiled.

"Emminghooaïe?" she repeated apologetically, lifting her eye-brows.

"Ernest, if it's easier."

"Ah, Ernest . . . Yes . . . I prefer Emminghooaïe," she proposed.

"And what shall I call you?" he chuckled.

"Devision."

"Not very Turkish, is this?"

"No, but Ottoman enough," she replied.

He leaned towards her, "That little boy by the bar, you know him?"

"Why?"

"He's been staring at me ever since I sat down."

"He thinks you're a ghost."

"Oh? Well, I have that effect on people I guess."

He guffawed.

"He thinks you look like his father. That's my brother. He is dead."

"Oh . . . I'm sorry."

"I told him I could pinch you to be sure."

"Go ahead, then."

She pinched his arm and turned to look at Niko, who looked away in embarrassment when the American winced.

The patrons had stopped teasing Constantine and were all staring at Elena, who appeared oblivious. Finally, Constantine went to the table and cleared his throat.

"Good evening, sir," he greeted the American in perfect English and without waiting for a response he turned to Elena and said, "I believe you are needed in the kitchen."

"Yes, I'm going," she said coolly and turned to the American, "Grazie."

When she entered the kitchen, Carmela was waiting for her, hands firmly planted on her enormous hips.

"What was that all about?"

Elena shrugged, "You mean people betting outside about getting a free drink?"

"No! You sitting down to have a drink with a perfect stranger."

"He invited me. He's a gentleman. Quite perfect, in that regard. What's the issue?"

Her curly mass of black hair, trapped in a net, shook from side to side like a grave pendulum with each gesture, as Carmela slid a few sardines into the frying pan.

"The issue is . . . respectable women do not drink with men, let alone perfect strangers. Period. Everyone was staring at you."

She dipped a sardine in flour and patted it dry. Her face was gleaming like a slippery sunset over the sea.

"Let them. I'm not doing anything wrong."

"But you are! Everyone will say you act like a . . . "

"Whore?"

"Everyone will talk."

"They will anyway. Did you need me to do something?"

She shrugged sullenly. Carmela showed her a pile of dirty dishes that needed washing. Elena sighed and rolled up her sleeves. She put the kettle on the stove to boil water for cleaning. "You're ruining your chances . . . " Her aunt started talking about Elena's lack of dowry and bon parti,* what everyone was saying about Marie's strange offspring and Niko's behaviour at school. Elena looked at the ceiling as she slipped her hands in the hot soapy water. After Carmela and Constantine had their fights and made peace, they turned their criticism to a third party, this time in unison, to cement their own precarious accord. Usually this party happened to be Marie's offspring, since they were around helping out most nights, and also because as uncle and aunt they felt they were entitled to criticize family members to whom they provided financial assistance. Elena felt the work she and Niko did for them amply

* prospective husband with money

repaid the assistance, but between labour and money, money carried greater weight.

When Elena left the kitchen, wiping the sweat off her forehead with her handkerchief, she noted with dismay that the American was gone. Niko was sleeping with his head resting on the bar counter, cushioned by his folded arms. She gently woke the boy and helped him get up. When they were out in the fresh night air, she took a deep breath and whistled for a horse carriage. Sitting in the swaying chamber, lulled by the monotonous clip-clop of the hooves, Niko went back to sleep. It was around eleven. Too late for a boy that age to be working anywhere. She would talk to her mother the next morning, tell her they would not go to Constantine's tavern any more. Her mother would get that worried expression. She decided not to speak of it yet.

They saw this Emminghooaïe a few times after that. He sat at the same spot with his pipe. Elena sketched his portrait from a few different angles, and offered him some of her sketches. Niko watched this from behind trays of sardines, glad the American was there to remind him of his father, and somewhat resentful that his aunt sat at the man's table, ate and drank with him, threw her head back and laughed insolently at his jokes.

Constantine observed the scene like a hawk. He was not pleased with his niece's behaviour and sent her to the kitchen as often as he could. In the end, he realized there was not much he could do, short of sending Elena and Niko home and telling them not to come back to the tavern. He did not want to do that, as he enjoyed their youthful presence around him. He secretly admired his little nephew's face as he sat pretending to do homework behind the bar, while gazing at faces and listening to conversations. He ruffled his hair with affection each time he passed him. He knew the boy was afraid of him, due to his size and the dark cellar beneath the tavern.

When the American did not come to the tavern, Elena would leave for a while, to take a walk and get fresh air. What no one figured was that she was meeting the American on the street and going for walks with him, away from everyone's gaze. He had told her he would be leaving in a few days. She took her jacket and left the tavern hurriedly, walking to the docks where the ship taking Emminghooaïe back to America was anchored. She walked back and forth waiting for him to arrive while a few sailors gathered on the ship's deck impassively observed the only woman around.

Emminghoaïe finally appeared just as she decided to walk away from the docks, thinking he had stood her up. After a handshake, they walked away from the sailors' gaze. She took him towards neighbourhoods where she was not likely to run into anyone familiar. She noticed that he was limping a little when they started walking up the hill. They advanced towards Mount Pagus, which overlooked the city, where Alexander was said to have cut the Gordian knot with his sword and ruled over Smyrna, Anatolia, and the rest of the world, she explained like a tour guide. It was a crisp winter evening. The sunset had smeared vermillion all over the sky and Mount Pagus now pierced it darkly with its crumbing castle walls surrounding it like a collar. They stood silently, breathing out little puffs of air, gazing at this view.

"The magical thing about this place . . . ," he started, turning around to take in the view of the bay with its scattered islands. He did not complete the sentence. Elena cut in, "Back in America perhaps you read Homer and history books about events far away, long ago, pages crowded with names you cannot even pronounce, and you're told it all relates to your world. Here, we live in that world; we breathe in it. The gods are still here, no matter how much the landscape changes. Agamemnon stood here, and Alexander, Tamerlane, and countless others; you read it in your books, but we see what they saw . . . In fact, we are, pretty much, what they saw."

She turned to him, cheeks flushed, suddenly realizing she had spoken condescendingly, but he nodded. "That's exactly what I was about to say."

They burst into laughter.

"If you stayed longer, I would take you to the place where Homer is said to have lived."

"Can we not go now?"

She shook her head. "It would take the whole day, and I would need to find an impossible excuse. Besides, you're leaving soon . . . "

"Tomorrow . . . "

They walked towards the castle ruins, and he told her of his work as an ambulance driver for the Red Cross in Italy, how he was wounded in the leg, which was the reason he was here, taking a short break before returning to America. Actually, he needed some time to himself.

"Before I leave, you have to get my name right. Say Hem . . . Come on, repeat!"

"Hem . . . "

" . . . ing like Heming."

"Heming."

"way."

"waï."

"No, wayy."

"Wayy."

"Right, say it."

"Hemingwayy."

"Good."

He shook her hand, holding hers in his a while longer. "I'm glad to have met you, Devision."

"You're pronouncing my name all wrong, Hemingway. It's not deh-vijn."

"Okay, then. Now that we have been properly introduced, tell me what you do when you're not working in that tavern and sketching faces."

"I paint."

"Then?"

"Then, nothing. I keep painting." She shrugged.

"No exhibitions?"

She burst into laughter.

"Are you mad? Who would buy a woman's paintings? Besides, I don't care about what they think."

"Get a man's name then. Why are you hiding?"

"How old are you, Hemingway?"

"Nineteen, why?"

"Why are you here?" she retorted. "Why the ambulance in Italy? Why anywhere but Chicago?"

"Because . . . " He thought for a moment, "Chicago is not enough, I guess."

"Ah? You see, for me, Smyrna is more than enough. Smyrna is too much. I hide from too much, you run from not enough. We are not so different."

She led him downhill. The night had wiped the red sunset from the sky, filling it with blackness and the flickering of stars. He was having difficulty going down with his limp. Elena took his arm, feeling the thickness of it through the jacket. He wrapped his free hand on hers as she grasped his arm to avoid slipping. She walked ahead of him slightly, her feet stepping around rocks to lead the way, her mind now off balance at the touch of his hand. Her fingers under his palm felt unrelated to the rest of her body. She wanted to let them rest there, for comfort. Yet a part of her wanted to withdraw immediately. Whenever her foot slipped over the gravel path, his grip tightened, so that as they arrived closer to the bottom of the hill, they were holding each other tighter than before. The smell of his cologne mixed with tobacco stirred her. She moved slightly away from his body to regain clarity. He cleared his throat.

"Are you all right?"

"Yes . . . fine."

"Thanks for taking me here. I will remember this view."

"You're welcome. I should go now; they must be wondering where I am." She extended her hand towards him, evading his gaze.

"I know the war is not over yet, here. It will be fought hard. And I may return sometime . . . "

He was speaking fast as if trying to be rid of the words. Elena was gazing at him, her head bent to the side, trying to understand what was coming next. He became quiet. She leaned close to his cheek, taking in the smell of his neck, and kissed him softly. It was her first kiss, cushioned with soft lips, warmed with mingling solitudes and lingering scents of sweet pipe tobacco. There were barriers of teeth and all those surmountable distances that bring the heart to one's mouth as an offering. She longed to remain there.

When she returned to the tavern, they were about to close the shutters. She apologized. Her uncle was silent. She figured this was not a good omen; he always became very quiet before bursting out in a thundering rage. Carmela was watching her every move, and understood something had happened that Constantine should never be told. To Elena's relief, there were no questions. She sat quietly in the carriage, gazing blankly at the empty streets and the starving dogs that wandered weightlessly through them. Niko's head, leaning heavily on her shoulder, was emitting gentle snores. She thought of the young American who would sail away the next morning, the boat fading from the harbour, leaving nothing behind except for the pipe which she occasionally felt through her coat pocket and the quickening pulse that had pushed her towards that kiss still thudding aimlessly in her bloodstream. She wondered how she would awaken to another Smyrnian morning, how her legs would carry what she now felt was an oversized and aching being through the chores of an hour, the streets of a city, and the small pleasures she never cared to name until this very moment. She did not yearn for the American to stay. She simply felt burdened by his departure, and by the uniqueness of an encounter which less abrupt lovers would tame through familiarity and repetition.

The following morning and in mornings to come, she walked to the quay to sketch the multitude of boats sitting in the sea like decoys. Day after day they anchored there, the fishing boats and the greater vessels, reassuring her that the harbour remained intact and the young American, many years her junior, who sailed away was an ethereal creature, a cloud that would rain elsewhere.

Meeting Mr Schmidt

LIFE RETURNED TO ITS USUAL rhythm after she had painted a dozen seascapes. Her scenes featured fishing boats, securely anchored, and cargo ships, their festive bodies still wet from the spray of the open seas, greater ships hovering in the horizon like ghosts from another world, and the cobblestone quay, gleaming with salty humidity at the edge of the turquoise water. In those who saw them, these paintings awakened a desire to spend their lives watching the sea from the quay, breathing the scent of iodine and algae with eyes squinting towards the horizon, where the sky only parted from the sea for a brief moment in the evenings to let the sun slip down like an egg yolk.

Neighbours and visitors to the house who had never noticed her paintings before, stopped in front of these new ones lined up in the hallway to enjoy them. She received a few requests, some even offered a nominal sum of money to walk away with them. Elena, baffled by the sudden attention, balked at parting from her paintings. She ruminated over Hemingway's advice to exhibit them under a man's name for a few weeks, until she finally walked down Rue de France to La Gallerie Schmidt, run by a German art dealer, with a few of her seascapes bundled into a large package under her arm.

Mr Schmidt, whose browless pale blue eyes and pointy nose did not match the plump red lips that nature had given him, sized her up and down as she nervously unbundled her offerings, feeling like a cheap peddler under his stern gaze. She uncovered the paintings and leaned them against the gallery wall, her heart thudding noisily in her ears. She was glad Mr Schmidt kept silent instead of asking her about herself.

The pale connoisseur walked back and forth, left arm strapped under his right forearm, whose extended hand cupped his chin. He did not seem to notice his own discomfort and Elena concluded it must have been a habitual contortion the man adopted for better concentration. He kept emitting "hmm," "ahh-zzo," and other unintelligible sounds, oblivious to Elena's growing unease. After what seemed like a very long muttering session in contorted body language, he walked to her and announced, "Commission only."

"Pardon?" Elena asked, startled.

"I will keep them on commission. If you sell, I'll take forty-five percent. I'll frame them too, of course. If you don't sell, you don't get paid. Agreed?"

Elena did not see any room for maneuvering, since she had no idea how galleries worked and had prepared herself to be sent home with a sneer.

"Agreed," the word came faintly out of her parched lips.

"Come back in ten days."

He steered her towards the gallery door, lacking the grace of a Smyrnian merchant, who would have offered tea or coffee first, taking the time to talk about a number of unrelated subjects with the purpose of establishing a relationship before getting down to business in an apologetic tangent. Mr Schmidt, she mused, as she left the gallery feeling somewhat insulted by his abruptness, belonged in Smyrna as much as his lips belonged on his face. The thought amused her as she walked home in her usual firm and hurried stride. She almost forgot her anxiety at having parted from her paintings.

She spent the next ten days at the hat shop with Polycarp, busying herself with the production of hats and dusting of mannequins, unable to go near her paint tubes and brushes. On day number ten, she ironed her only other dress and wore it with care to pay her second visit to the gallery. At nine o'clock she left the house carrying her umbrella and a purse, which was empty except for an embroidered handkerchief. She took a detour to the gallery, walking on the quay to get a glimpse of the sea that shone like a steel plate under an overcast sky. Pigeons and seagulls took flight at the slightest provocation, only to return to the boy who was throwing food at them, his feet dangling from the sea wall. The boy was in school uniform, his school bag and jacket beside him; his metal lunch box was open, the food serving as bird feed. She was about to approach but changed her mind and advanced hurriedly towards the gallery.

When she pushed the door open, she expected to see Mr Schmidt there, his stern gaze fixed on her person. He was nowhere to be seen. The gallery was lined with beautifully framed works, and the marble floor was laid with long red carpets guiding one's steps from one painting to the next. She walked around observing them, which she had not dared to do before. There were watercolour landscapes, fresh and masterly, signed by Doumanian, an oil painting representing Alpine glaciers by P Leroux, a portrait of a child done awkwardly, in the manner of Renoir. She arrived at one of her own paintings, placed in a beautifully handcrafted frame. She was filled with a sense of glee. She moved back, to see it with the eyes of a stranger, when she bumped into someone. It was Mr Schmidt. Embarrassed, she mumbled an absurd apology.

Mr Schmidt was smiling. "You like the way it looks?"

She nodded, caught off guard by his beaming smile. Putting his hand on her arm, Mr Schmidt gently guided her towards his desk, where he motioned her to a leather armchair.

"You should be," he said.

"I should be . . . ?"

"Proud, yes? You have sold three of the four already. I have never seen anything like this. I don't know if it's beginners' luck or what." He reached for an envelope in a drawer.

"Here is your share," he extended it to her. "Please count it before leaving, to be sure."

"Oh no, no . . . need," she bleated in embarrassment. "I'm sure you've done a fine job of it."

She didn't know where to look so as not to stare at the envelope, which in fact was all she wanted to do. Her tongue, a slab of concrete in her mouth. She sprang up to end her discomfort and looked towards the door.

"Sit down, please," cautioned Mr Schmidt, gently.

"Would you like some water or tea?"

She nodded. He walked over to a table where a jug of water stood beside a few overturned glasses. As he poured the water, he turned to her.

"Now, about the future. . . The remaining painting is also about to go. A certain Mr Van der Meer was interested in it and said he would pass by. Do you know him?"

She nodded as she took a big gulp. It made her cough. Water sprayed on her dress and Mr Schmidt's crimson pout parted into a smile. She wanted to run for the door.

Mr Schmidt said kindly, "I know you're disbelieving the whole thing. But it is true. I would like you to bring me more of your paintings, and let's see how it goes."

She smiled back after regaining her composure and nodded. "That would be fine. I have some paintings I can bring you."

"I never thought I would encounter a woman painter in Smyrna. Where did you learn this?"

She shrugged. "Nowhere. Copying masters. I've learned mostly from them, I suppose."

Mr Schmidt's small blue eyes narrowed as if trying to understand something that was not apparent, while his lips formed into a disconnected smile meant to continue the conversation.

"Very well, Miss Devision. You can pass by in three days with the other paintings you want to show me. We can talk further then."

She sprang up, clutching the envelope, which she realized she should hide in her purse. She extended her hand for a handshake, and walked to the door, where she finally managed to clumsily stuff the envelope into her little handbag and left the shop.

Niko Makes a Wish

NIKO WATCHED HER SKIP from the corner of the street all the way to the house. He was home with the mumps. He did not believe his cheeks and jaw would ever return to their old state, since he could not even remember how they looked before he got so swollen. Elena opened the door and banged it shut, causing her mother to make noises about the need for lady-like behaviour from the kitchen. She ran up to the attic, motioning to Niko to follow her. She sat him across from her and opened her purse to take out the crumpled envelope, which she tore open. She took out the bills and counted them, her eyes gleaming.

"What would you like to have?"

He shrugged.

"Come on, tell me, what do you really really want to have right now?"

Niko half whispered, "A bicycle."

Elena giggled. "You wait for me. I'll be right back."

She stuffed the money into her purse and ran down the stairs, slamming the door again, causing more grumbling in the kitchen.

The boy returned to his room and began to wait. He had no energy to invent games due to his fever and yet he felt he needed to find a way to keep busy while Elena was away. He could not sit still or look out the window. He buttoned and unbuttoned his cardigan, stretched himself on the bed; hoping to fall asleep he tossed and turned and picked up a book and put it down; he imagined a soccer game in which he scored a goal to everyone's awe. When he looked at the time again, only ten minutes had passed. He wanted to cry. Elena was nowhere in sight. He imagined her walking to Peregrini's toy store where he hoped she would choose the blue bicycle he saw everyday in the shop window on his way to school. What if it was already sold? He agonized for an eternity before he sat in front of the window looking at his distorted reflection once again.

Elena finally appeared, riding the blue bicycle in the middle of the street. Its chrome handlebars were gleaming in the sun. Niko shrieked with joy, ran down the stairs and out to the street. Marie, who could not understand what the door-bangings were about, walked out of the house to see her grandson (who a few hours before was moaning with fever) riding a bicycle in circles. He stopped feeling again the pain in his cheeks, got off and rushed to his aunt and hugged her. He stood there hugging her quietly until Elena felt his sobs bursting onto her chest.

That night they ate roast beef, potatoes, and pilaf, rinsed down with a glass of wine (diluted with water for Niko), to celebrate Elena's unexpected earnings. They were all spent on the bicycle and the dinner. They ate silently at the table, which was set with Hungarian porcelain and Italian crystals arranged with the greatest care on the starched white tablecloth, their cheeks glowing with pleasure for the first time since the disappearance of Jacob. Elena turned to Polycarp with an enigmatic smile. "You are right. There is no such thing as coincidence." She thought of her brother Jacob, the American who resembled him, the kiss she had enjoyed, and finally the paintings, which had brought on this very moment when Jacob's presence was felt as though he had returned transformed, never to be torn from their midst again.

Niko fell asleep sated, admiring his new bicycle, which his grandmother had allowed him to carry up the stairs to his bedroom. When he opened his eyes in the dark, at the end of a dream, his father was sitting at the foot of his bed, gazing at him. Niko felt his pulse accelerate. He could not utter a sound. "I came to see how you were," said his father, and placed his hand gently on the boy's foot, which did not budge under the covers. "Nice bicycle. Enjoy it, my boy," he said, as he rose and leaned over to kiss Niko's forehead. Niko felt the warmth of the kiss on his skin. Then his father straightened his back and walked towards the bedroom door where he vanished.

When he came downstairs for breakfast and told his grandmother what he saw in the night, she crossed herself repeatedly and wanted to know the details of Jacob's attire, his facial expression, his exact words, and was not satisfied until the boy had repeated it all at least three times. Finally she sighed and caressed the boy's head. "When the departed return, it is always to tell you something important. Now you know he is watching over you. You'll never be lonely again."

She took out her handkerchief to rub her eyes dry.

The Secret Life of Manolis

NIKO COULD HARDLY WAIT to go to school again. He planned to take his bicycle and, at last, join his other friends who gathered every day on a field to have races. These boys came from rich families and always had the newest toys. This once he would have the newest thing, the most beautiful and shiny, even if he sometimes went to school without underwear and wore folded sheets of newspaper inside his shoes to cover holes. The morning he was finally able to leave the house with normal-sized cheeks, he proudly pedaled down the street, his old leather school bag swinging from the handlebars. He was whistling joyously as he neared Manolis's house. Manolis was standing on his small front porch in his housecoat, with perfectly combed raven hair, sipping a small cup of Turkish coffee. Niko could smell the thick fragrance even from a distance. He waved to Manolis, who waved back. "Is it new? Come, show me."

Happy to oblige, Niko got off the bicycle and brought it over for a detailed inspection. Manolis squeezed the tires and checked the brakes expertly. He nodded to show his admiration. "That's a very good one! Where did you get it?"

"My aunt got it at Peregrini's."

"Excellent. How is your aunt these days? And your grandma? And your uncle, of course . . . "

"They're all fine. You should visit!"

He got on his bicycle and rode off. Manolis continued sipping his coffee, wondering how Elena got the money to buy a new bicycle, when the family struggled to have one decent meal. He had decided to stay away for a while, noticing that Elena had become distant since she started going to the quay to paint her boats. What a strange obsession for a beautiful woman like her, he mused. Another would do her utmost to find a rich husband, spend her days parading on the quay to attract the best. Not Elena. She thought nothing of walking in the streets with her clothes covered with paint stains and her boots falling apart. She would forget to eat unless food was brought to her. She could spend the entire day not saying a word to anyone. He smiled, she would make the worst possible wife. There would be no meals, he would have to iron his own shirts and probably her dresses too. She would have impressed neither of his parents had they been alive, nor anyone else he knew. The question of whether their children would be raised as Catholics or Orthodox Greeks was an absurd one. Yet the mere look of her sent his heart racing. And this, from the time he was a boy. He used to admire the way she climbed trees, or told everyone what to do, the way her socks were always loose around her ankles, showing bruised and scraped legs, her hair bunched in a semblance of pigtails dangling unevenly on each side of her face. When she observed things, she had a way of putting both her fists on her hips. These memories continued to delight him now when he looked at the woman she had become. He had loved her since he remembered loving. And he had no idea how to proceed, what to offer, where to fit in her unfamiliar world. He was a practical man. Always knew he would take care of people; a wife, children, patients. A life of morning coffee, newspaper, and clinic, followed by evenings at home and family gatherings on weekends. This was the life he wanted. Instead, he had a dog for company, patients that kept him busy, and in the evenings, underground work for an organization that was inspired by Venizelos's Megalo Idea of reconquering Byzantium. He wanted to help Greece have her share of the crumbling Ottoman Empire; not so much because of his love for Greece, which was not his land, but because of profound angst he felt at the end of this devastating war, in which so much had been lost and destroyed, facing the disappearance of a way of life that had defined this ancestral home for centuries. He was neither Greek nor Turk, but Anatolian. He was part of the mass known as Rum for centuries. After the World War there were winners and losers, nations rising, others crumbling, with the great players of Europe advancing their own interests over the lands that were once the Ottoman Empire, like vultures circling over a carcass. He had to choose Greece, but found it distasteful to dwell on his clandestine activities, preferring instead to push them into the dark cloak of the night, so he would not observe himself feeling conflicted.

As he took another sip of his coffee, he mused that his life made no sense; he loved a woman he could not fathom, and worked for a cause not truly his own. Could the woman love him back, and could the cause safeguard what he did not want to lose? What actually pushed him to start his practice in Smyrna was the organization. They told him they needed someone to work inside Smyrna to prepare for the invasion. He left Salonica in a hurry, taking his leave from a heartbroken fiancée to come and live beside Elena. It would all make sense if she loved him back one day.

He walked back into the house, placed the cup of coffee on the kitchen counter, and sat down to read the newspapers. He was unable to concentrate, his mind tugging back towards Elena and the meaning of his actions. He rose to get dressed and as he prepared to leave the house, clutching his leather bag, half an hour later, he had made the firm decision to pay her a visit the following evening. Instead of going to his clinic, he strolled towards the port area. He had to organize secret meetings to take place in an old spice factory. He had found the men for the job, now he had to organize the operation. This would easily take him the entire day.

When the sun rose the next morning, he hurried to his clinic, which was in Kemeraltı, the ancient marketplace where everything was sold, from evil-eye beads to horseshoes, cloth, and spices. The area was flanked on one side by Kızlarağası, the ancient building where girl slaves had been sold in past centuries, and by a mosque on the other, with criss-crossing narrow streets that were sheltered from rain and sun by spreading vines. The light came down filtered here through the thick foliage. There was a constant shuffling of feet, raising the aroma of spices and herbs that had rubbed into the stones over centuries. Everywhere you went you could hear the tinkling of tiny spoons in tea glasses shaped like a woman. The deep, plaintive voice of a man singing a *mâné*, a sad love song, came from a distant and muted gramophone as the call to the morning prayer came down from the minaret. "Allaaahüekber!" the müezzin's voice meandered through the streets. Manolis closed his eyes in the midst of this sensual feast, letting the call to prayer vibrate through his body. The beauty of it, he realized, came from the melancholy submission it evoked, to the impenetrable ways of destiny and life. As he listened, he heard the solitary struggle that precedes surrender in the man's voice, as if he had grappled with the great questions of life all night long and finally, at dawn, was crying out for help. It wasn't in the words, which he did not understand, but in their delivery. Beauty was what burned his heart in the middle of this cobblestone alley in Kemeraltı.

When he arrived at his clinic on the second floor of an old wooden house at the top of a creaking flight of stairs, there were already three people waiting for him. One was Kona Loksandra, a hypochondriac in her fifties who needed her weekly reassurance that she was gravely ill but would live to be a hundred. The other two were a mother and son. It was the ten-year-old who needed his care. His face was pale and moist, his eyes glassy in their dark sockets. His left fist was wrapped around a wooden soldier. He did not need to examine the boy to know he suffered from consumption and would most likely die within the year. Greeting his patients politely, he invited them inside as he disappeared behind a door to come out a few moments later in a white coat, a stethoscope round his neck. His waiting room was decorated with a single painting. Elena's *Venice,* with the blind accordion player in the gondola of doom. It served to put out whatever glimmer of hope his patients felt as they waited to be examined. Still, it was Elena's *Venice,* and there it would hang.

At the end of his work day, he returned home in a state of agitation, to get ready for his visit. He heated up water in a large cauldron to wash himself in the kitchen, where the water drained through a screened hole in the floor. He ironed his shirt and trousers with some difficulty, making a mental note to look for a housekeeper, and was finally perfumed and ready. He walked over to Elena's house, having eaten bread and cheese so he could say he had already supped, to spare them the discomfort of offering him food they could not spare. He brought along a box of chocolates a patient had given him. The door was opened by Marie. Delighted by his visit, she hugged and kissed him before showing him to the living room, and called out to the family to come down and greet him.

They all gathered downstairs. Marie began to explain to him with embellishments Elena's success at the gallery. Elena cut in with the short version. Manolis was impressed. He got up to congratulate Elena with a hug, promising to visit the gallery the next day. His nose brushed the tiny curls of soft hair on the side of her neck. His eyes fell on the chiselled pout of her lips. Unable to stand her closeness, he left, explaining he needed to do things at home.

Outside, he recalled that he meant to tell her he had found the coin she had tossed long ago from the window upstairs. He had dug in his backyard and found it wrapped in red cloth, surpised that the earth hadn't eaten up this most vivid souvenir. He had sat there, soil pressed under his fingernails, staring at the old copper coin and the bed of sticks he had made for it on that hot summer afternoon, but he was unable to make the boy who had done this return. He had uncovered the memory but not the moment. That, he observed, had been chewed up by time.

When Elena shut the door and returned to the cold living room, she knew Polycarp would have a comment, and he did.

"He'll go and buy everything at the gallery to impress you. He'll ruin himself just to get your attention, you know."

Elena looked at her brother, not understanding.

He continued, rolling his eyes, "Of course, you thought he was coming to see me . . . " He waited for a comment, which did not come, and he shrugged, turning the page of his book.

Marie threw in, "He obviously likes you. And he has a good position. I'm sure he has wood for his stove."

"Mama!" Elena exclaimed.

Marie thought it wise to drop the subject at this point, while Elena was still merely annoyed. One notch higher, and she would blow like a hurricane. Why was Elena so stubborn about securing a comfortable life through a good marriage? She imagined her daughter's future as a dried-up maid who would eventually be forced to work as a governess for spoiled children, or as a companion for a rich old demented woman, ending up finally as an old woman herself, childless, alone, and poor. She sighed, resolving to bring up the subject later, lay the sad facts on the table, on one of Elena's more reasonable days.

Outside, Manolis was walking in the dark streets, the occasional gas lamp lighting a large circle around its post. The city seemed like a foreign place, full of strangers at night. There were furtive noises of stray cats going through garbage; people walked alone, or in pairs, bits of conversation hung in the cold air. A wave of melancholia swept through him. Everyone on the street, even the stray cats, seemed imbued with purpose while he remained vacant. Turning a corner, he arrived at the Quay, where rows of giant palm trees stood facing a black and motionless sea. One could hear only the gentle lapping of water on the wall. Echoes of dance music came from the distant clubs and restaurants along the Quay. He was already near La Punta, a working-class neighbourhood at the edge of the harbour, where the land jutted out to the sea. He passed the Maltese taverns, whose steamed windows blocked all view, and the warehouses with long shadows, and the townhouses with small windows.

He arrived at his destination, a spice factory where thyme, oregano, and bay leaves were purified before export. He entered and walked towards the small, poorly lit office in the back where half a dozen men were having a heated debate in Greek. They greeted him vaguely and continued their conversation. Manolis, who organized and ran these meetings, moved to the head of the table and cleared his throat, effectively putting an end to the debate. Thereafter, only his voice was heard, explaining the plan of action and questioning the individuals on their respective tasks. A shipment of arms was due to arrive from the island of Chios. One of the men had to be in Çeşme, the coastal village, to receive it and ship it to Smyrna where it would be distributed through the Greek-Orthodox church of Aya Katerina. He assigned the task of carrying the shipment to the city to two of the men. The other two were to distribute the arms during mass on two consecutive Sundays. They agreed on the time and place of the next meeting. He had conducted the twenty minutes of this meeting standing up, without removing his coat, and now that the business was concluded he took his leave politely and left the building, hands in his pockets. The men were assured of his indifference to them, which he projected through a businesslike and calculating demeanor. He never participated in their political debates or inquired about their personal lives, addressing them by their surnames, using the plural form of "you," thus discouraging any illusion of intimacy. His partners had nicknamed him "Greek Ice," assuming he was from mainland Greece, sent to run the operation from the top.

As he left the building, Manolis noticed the smell of oregano and thyme following him out, already imbued into his coat. He would have to take another bath in the freezing kitchen and hang his coat to air out on the balcony tonight. He wondered what Elena would be doing at this hour. He had got in the habit of passing her on his way back from meetings. The light was usually on in the attic and he would go to bed thinking of her still painting.

Elena's Contract

AT MIDNIGHT, AS MANOLIS was passing under her window looking up at it, Elena was slumped in her armchair in the attic staring
at the business card that Mr Schmidt had given her the day before.

Mr A Van der Meer
Van der Meer & Son Shipping Co

The address was in Pasaport, near the Customs Office. The Van
der Meers were an old Smyrnian family of Dutch origin. They had
been in the shipping business since the early seventeenth century,
when Sultan Süleyman the Magnificent invited foreigners to settle
in the Empire and conduct business, free of tax and on their own
terms, as a magnanimous if shortsighted gesture of goodwill and
generosity. Businessmen and bankers arrived from all corners of
Europe, and farmers and craftsmen from the Balkan provinces and
Greece, to settle in the wealthy cities of Izmir and Istanbul and the
fertile Aegean coast. Dutchmen began their shipping business, the
Italians exported dried figs, the French built hospitals and schools,
the Belgians set up the waterworks, and so it went, for centuries.

Van der Meer, one of the wealthiest men in Izmir, was also an art
lover, whose mansion in Cordelio was filled with the most beautiful paintings and sculptures. Cordelio* was a rich suburb on the

* now named Karşıyaka

68

north side of the bay, where every house had its own beach and extensive grounds that required a groundskeeper. The Van der Meer garden was reputed to have the loveliest roses in Smyrna, though very few people had actually seen it. The man whose card she held in her hands was a bachelor in his early forties who had recently taken over the family business from his ailing father. A rather eccentric man, he kept mostly to himself and spoke Turkish to everyone no matter how they addressed him, even though he was fluent in the other languages. Levantines in Izmir spoke French in public, Greek at home, and Turkish when they went grocery shopping or for bureaucratic reasons.

The next morning Elena went to Pasaport and looked for the address on the card. When she entered the building, a stout, moustachioed man in a fez holding amber prayer beads walked up to her quickly.

"Müsyü Van der Meer, please," she requested.

"Müsyü Van der Meer is away. He will return next month. He's retired, actually."

"I'm looking for the son."

"One moment." The man, with a mocking twinkle in his eyes, nodded and shuffled towards an office, opened the door and spoke to someone inside. Van der Meer appeared in the doorway to take a look at Elena. He whispered something to the man, who returned to her, now sizing her up with an arrogant smile that flashed a golden tooth. "Müsyü Van der Meer is very busy and would like to know what it is about . . . "

"I'm the painter. He knows," she cut in icily.

When the befezzed man with his insolent tooth returned once more to give his boss the message, Van der Meer reappeared in the doorway with a bewildered look. He walked towards Elena with the bouncy gait of an athlete and extended his hand.

"Madame . . . "

" . . . demoiselle."

"What can I do for you?"

Elena, without trying to dissimulate her irritation, declared, "You told Mr Schmidt you wanted to meet me. Now kindly explain why you wanted to see me, or I will leave as I have much to do today!"

She turned slightly, ready to go. Her eyes were wide open and stern. Van der Meer, a thin, grey-eyed man in a navy blue suit, apologized immediately and invited her into his office. Elena sensed the doorman's eyes on her back as the door closed.

Her paintings of the harbour were hanging on three walls and she was impressed. There were wooden maquettes of sailboats in large bottles on the windowsill. She felt uncomfortable. Mr Van der Meer ("Call me Pieter, please, it's faster") went to great lengths to explain his awe at the luminosity of her paintings and how sea-scapes and ships were so evocative, hers especially, and his surprise at her being a woman yet such a fabulous painter. She could see he meant well.

"You mean to say," she interrupted tersely, "that being a woman and a good painter are not compatible."

It was Van der Meer's turn to be embarrassed. He hastened to apologize for not expressing himself clearly. She glanced at his grandfather clock quickly, making him understand that it was time to state the reason for her visit. Mr Schmidt had mentioned that she was good at copying the masters, he started. He had some masters in mind from his ancestral corner of the world that he wanted her to copy, Ruisdael, Vermeer, and Brueghel the Elder, to name a few. He had books with pictures, and if she was inclined to accept, they could look at them together, to choose her first commission. Elena felt queasy but she nodded. She asked to see the Brueghel reproductions. Her tongue felt thick and dry. She looked at *Wedding Banquet*, the warm light on the faces of the guests and kitchen help, and said she'd start with it. He removed the reproduction and gave it to her. He was ready to pay a handsome sum for each copy, and no matter how queasy she felt, this meant they could buy wood for the stove and have decent food.

After the handshakes and niceties that in the Smyrnian manner went on for half an hour while standing by the doorway, she left the building only to be called back by Van der Meer, who had rushed after her, waving an envelope in his hand. He was slightly out of breath. "First instalment. It'll help buy the materials."

The befezzed doorman, who was sitting by, no longer felt any need to hide his covetous gaze as he freely sized her up and down.

"Please tell your employee to stop oggling me. I will decline your commission should he stare at me next time I come." She said this very quietly and walked away, leaving him perplexed.

Elena turned a corner and stood there, breathless with fear. She took out the envelope and looked inside. There was more money than she had ever seen. She took out the folded reproduction from her handbag, feeling doubtful she could manage the task she had accepted. "A woman, yet such a fabulous painter," she remembered, and wondered if she might have accepted the commission out of resentment. She would go home and sit with the picture for a while before declining the work. She stuffed the money back into her pocket and proceeded towards the marketplace called Pazar, or Sunday. Today was Wednesday, Ayşe's dandelion day. Elena wanted potato moussaka with ground beef. Surely she could borrow a few kurush from the envelope to buy meat and potatoes. She would find a way to replace the money before bringing it back to Van der Meer.

She quickened her steps towards the noisy market, farmers singing out from their stalls. Not that there was much variety any more, or that many customers. "We sell potatoes, onions, garlic, and caaauliflower too-oo!" She bought a few potatoes and half a dozen bunches of wild violets. The newspaper wrapping in Arabic script announced postwar peace negotiations were underway in Paris. The Ottoman Empire had fallen, alongside its German partner. The newspaper bemoaned the unfortunate alliance and questioned the future of the sultanate. The cold January winds from the north seared her red hands as she hurried home.

Elena sat in her old armchair in the attic, gazing at *Peasant Wedding:* the jugs in the left hand corner, the man pouring water or wine from a larger metal jug into small ceramic ones, the plump child with the look of a midget and wearing a red hat, licking her fingers having finished her soup, the warm colours of her clothing, the red-nosed bagpipe player staring hungrily at the plates of soup being carried on a platter, the soft and comfortable shoes of the waiters, the buzz of good-natured conversation you could almost hear round the table, the peasant bride smiling contentedly to herself as everyone around her busied themselves feasting, the cozy feel of indoors in winter, the light from an invisible fireplace reflected on faces and objects. She sat observing each and every detail of the painting before going to her table to cut a small square window in the middle of a paper sheet. She moved the window around on the reproduction, forming each time an exquisitive miniature, wondering how Brueghel the Elder had succeeded in creating this cohesion of small masterpieces into a larger and perfectly harmonious composition of colours and shapes. She went to stretch the canvas and nail it over a wooden frame, asking for Brueghel's forgiveness, and thanked him for being so good that she would never be able to copy him well. Once she had the canvass ready, she drew vertical and horizontal lines on the reproduction with a pencil and copied the same lines on the canvas. She started drawing with a pencil the figures and shapes on her canvas, using the squares for accuracy. She then put a thin base of very light pinkish yellow on the entire canvas, to rid it of whiteness. Copying Brueghel meant she had to learn to see like him, and to use her fingers and wrists like him, to mix colours as he did. It was a monumental task.

The next morning she went to Clementini's and ordered a book on Brueghel. A regular at his store, she had become friends with the bookseller, who let her sit inside and read books without buying them. She spent the rest of the day reading. Clementini, whose thick grey hair flew around his head like a pigeon only to be secured into a small goatee under his chin, was a thin, rather concave man with a small torso. His legs seemed to start right below the diaphragm. When someone asked him for a book, his piercing brown eyes hovered in the air before settling on a direction. He then marched to the exact spot and found it in the labyrinth that was his small store, with narrow aisles and columns of books everywhere. He knew all the editions, whether he had a particular one or not, and exactly where it hid among the mountains of leather and paper.

When the rich ladies in bucket hats came in looking for something "pour faire passer le temps," he invariably sold them *Anna Karenina* or *Madame Bovary*, both of which he seemed to carry in unlimited supply. The hat store was not far from Clementini's. Elena had clued in to his perverse humour and would smile from behind the columns of books. He once sold Marquis de Sade's *Justine* to a balding accountant, who asked him for a book "to erase the numbers from my mind before going to sleep at night."

Elena left the store that cold winter evening, meaning to go home, but ended up on the Quay instead. Grey boats, grey sea, grey pigeons, whiffs of iodine. Palm trees, tall impassive witnesses to an ever changing view. What will become of us, Elena thought, feeling her chest narrow around her heart. This living by the sea like insects in the sand, never going into the water and never moving inland. Zigzagging back and forth on the shore in search of dried sea things. The sea swelling up in its grey fury to wash it all away. More dried-up sea things, for a new generation of witless insects zigzagging in the dunes. She felt the wave coming closer, and life as she knew it would soon be washed away. Somewhat incoherently she intuited why Brueghel was important for her to copy, at that precise moment. The world did not need another copy of *Banquet*, but Elena needed to hold on to its wisdom, to learn what Brueghel knew, and to remain afloat.

When she returned to her attic, she felt peaceful and content, like someone preparing to meet a beloved friend. Niko was there, doing his homework on the floor in a corner, in the flickering light of the portable gas lamp. He was crouched, his feet crossed behind, his heels glowing pink through the holes in his socks. She cherished the spheres of skin for the fleeting tenderness they aroused in her gaze. Brueghel the Elder was all around.

The Dilemma

THE SUN ROSE FROM BEHIND the hills of Aya Yorghi near the town of Çeşme, shining its first rays of crude wintery light into the eyes of the two men waiting for the arms shipment from the island of Chios. A horsecart filled with bales of hay and hemp sacks stood beside them. The grey horse swayed his tail left and right. Squinting, the men looked west, to the wide expanse of the sea. Costa lifted the binoculars to his eyes once again. Antoni threw his rolled cigarette down, squeezing the tobacco out of its paper in a few nervous twists of his shoe.

"They were supposed to be here before sunrise. I don't know how we'll do this if they're any later."

"Relax, will you?" replied Costa, looking compulsively through the binoculars before turning to his friend. "There's not a soul here beside us."

"If the gendarmes see us . . . " Antoni made a throat-slitting gesture.

The bells of Aya Yorghi started tolling in the distance.

"We've done the same thing dozens of time, aren't you used to it yet?"

"We've never done it in broad daylight! I don't have a good feeling about this. We've been standing here since three o'clock. Nothing's moving. Let's get out of here."

"What if the boat arrives?"

"We'll go to town and telegraph Mr Ice. Maybe he knows some-thing. The boat should have been here three hours ago. Maybe they got caught. Let's get out of here before they come looking for us."

Antoni got on the horsecart. "Are you coming?" he urged Costa who squinted at the sea one more time before reluctantly joining his friend. They went straight to the post office when they entered the town.

AUNT PANAGIOTA DID NOT COME. IS SHE SICK?

When Manolis received the telegram, he was in his clinic with a patient. He told the man with the swollen tonsils that he had urgent business to attend to and advised everyone in the waiting room to come back the next day. He ignored the sighs and grumbles as he locked the door to his clinic and rushed away. As he walked he glanced around a few times to see if he was followed. He pushed open the wrought-iron gate to a well-kept garden and walked up the path to the house where a housekeeper greeted him. He slipped in and was led to an ornate dining room where the businessman who was his local contact, assigned to him by the organization in Athens, was having his coffee. As Manolis entered, the man's wife finished her coffee and left the room discreetly. Manolis hoped to possibly get some answers here. The businessman was one of the players expected to lead the political scene once Smyrna became Greek. He had a grave voice and a white moustache which he occa-sionally twirled as he spoke.

He explained to Manolis that they suspected their cover in Çeşme had been blown and had diverted the shipment to the island of Mit-ilini at the last minute, from where it had already passed to Ayvalık on the mainland, and would arrive at the Church of Aya Katerina late at night. Time, he explained, was running out. No one was sure how the information had leaked, but at this point there was no time for a full investigation. He cautioned Manolis to keep an eye on his men and report to him before Sunday.

Manolis felt bothered as he left. If one of his five men had betrayed them, it would be his task to deal with him. He sweated profusely as he walked aimlessly in the streets, trying to focus on what needed to be done. Although he was not under direct pressure to find the culprit, he understood that he was expected to do something or he would be under suspicion himself. He walked into an alley to vomit. Feeling somewhat relieved, he worked out a rudimentary plan. He stepped into the post office to phone the businessman and asked for four reliable men whom he would meet at night in secret. He was assured the four men would meet him where he asked. Manolis then phoned his office boy to call on his five men to ask them to meet him at a tavern at La Punta the following evening. Then he hurried home. He wanted to bury his head in a pillow, empty his mind, rest. He was frightened. His heart was thudding in his chest and he could hardly stand on his weakened legs. As he walked towards his house, chin tucked into his chest, he heard someone call his name and jumped.

"It's just me!" said Pol, shocked to see his friend's face so drawn and haggard. "What's wrong with you?"

Manolis shrugged. "I'm fine. Just a bit of stomach problem. Must have been something I ate. I'll rest a bit, that's all I need."

He lifted his hand to wave goodbye and climbed the steps to his porch and entered his house.

He sighed deeply as he closed the door behind him, annoyed at being seen in such a state. Why did I get myself into this, his mind repeatedly questioned in a useless loop. Why am I doing this? He collapsed on the sofa and closed his eyes. A horrific image played itself beneath his closed eyes. He was shooting a man through his coat pocket. The man fell with an accusing glare before turning into a dead heap. Manolis plunged into a deep slumber.

The next evening he walked to the tavern to meet his five men. He had chosen the tavern so he could shed his cold image somewhat by buying the men drinks to make them feel at ease. He had met the other four men at the park by the synagogue the night before and instructed them to take up positions by the tavern. They were to follow four of the men secretly for the next couple of days and report to him. He himself would follow the fifth one, who would come out with him.

He felt once again in control of the situation as he pushed the tavern door open. He had dressed down to blend in with his men, wearing casual clothes and a cap. Smoke swirled above the crowded tables, making it difficult to see. A man waved at him. He walked towards the table, greeting them all as he sat down. They had already finished their first round of ouzo. He called the waiter and ordered a bottle for the table, and the men quickly glanced at each other in surprise. Greek Ice was melting.

"To a job well done!" Manolis raised his glass and they followed suit, not quite understanding what he meant. "We're done for now. We won't need to meet again. Everything is taken care of. It's been a success, thanks to you all." He took a gulp. They imitated him, still confused.

Costa asked, "What happened in Aya Yorghi?"

Antoni said, "We waited five hours on the beach. We could have been nailed."

"But nothing happened. No further shipments were deemed necessary, and they did not have time to warn us in advance. In any case, no worries now, right?" Manolis smiled round the table, "Our part is done. Time to sit back and wait."

Antoni asked, somewhat uneasily, "What is going to happen now?"

"I don't know," replied Manolis. "I just know that our part is complete. It's best not to know, anyway, this way, if we're caught, we have nothing to cough up. Don't you agree?"

Antoni shook his head yes and took another sip of his drink.

Spiro, who had nicknamed him Greek Ice, offered, "We didn't realize you were . . . like us. We thought you didn't care."

"I apologize," said Manolis. "I wasn't comfortable socializing when there was so much to be done. But now it's different . . . "

He waved at the waiter, who came up hurriedly from the other side of the tavern, a pencil stuck behind his ear.

"Bring us some fried calamari, bread, feta . . . mézés." He leaned over to fill the men's glasses once more.

The men seemed reluctant to treat Manolis as one of their own, until the food came and they started eating. Mézés accompanied by copious amounts of ouzo, however, succeeded in removing the barriers of class and upbringing that were very much there at the beginning of the evening. They laughed more easily as the evening progressed, and it was one AM when they left the tavern arm in arm, singing, "Yalo, Yalo."

They walked out into the night. A window opened and a man's head popped out, cursing. They resumed walking quietly after that, until one by one they took their leave, ready to return home and get scolded by their wives. Antoni, younger than the rest, did not have a wife and asked Manolis if he wanted to go with him. Manolis agreed.

"I'll take you to the House with the Piano," Antoni winked. Manolis tried to wink back. He had no idea what this meant. "Have you ever been?" pressed Antoni, who seemed to be more in control of his faculties.

"No. Is it another tavern?" slurred Manolis.

Antoni emitted a horsey laugh. "It's a whorehouse, you fool!"

Manolis shook his head. "I don't think I can find it even to pee. Everything's numb." He looked down at his pants.

"It's a good walk. You'll feel better by then! You're paying, though. I can't afford it."

Manolis nodded. Antoni continued, "It's famous. Generals and rich men go there . . . If you have the money, we can be generals for one night, eh? Are you sure you have enough money?"

Manolis nodded. "I think so. I'll pay for you anyway. I'll just watch. I don't think I can use this idiot at all." He looked down at his pants once again, perplexed.

"Like hell, you watch!"

"Fine, then. I'll take a nap in the waiting room. How far is this place, anyway?"

They walked arm in arm in the sleeping city, occasionally stumbling as they stepped up and down sidewalks to cross the streets. In the crisp night air Manolis began slowly to focus better. They arrived in Kokaryalı, the Jewish residential neighbourhood south of Smyrna, with its stone houses and fragrant rose gardens. Manolis of course had been there the day before. He wondered if the other four men were being followed and what this investigation would turn up. Antoni, whom he had started suspecting at the tavern due to his pointed questions about the operation, seemed to him now a foolish young man in pursuit of uncomplicated thrills. A whorehouse. He shook his head, smiling. Antoni gave him a sidelong glance. "What are you smiling about? Feeling less numb, are you?"

"Do you think they're open at this hour?" wondered Manolis.

"All night. I already know the one I want. Her name's Despina."

"You said you'd never been there!"

"Haven't. But everybody knows about her. Except you. The most beautiful woman in Smyrna. They even sing about her."

"Do you think we can afford her?" asked Manolis, thinking his fact-finding expedition was turning into a costly farce.

"You can," asserted Antoni.

They arrived in front of a beige two-storey house that looked no different than the others from outside. They went up the steps and knocked. Instead of the usual gargoyle, the brass knocker represented a nude beauty with long flowing hair. The door was opened by a woman in her late fifties, dressed in a red décolleté gown, her crumpled bluish-white flesh squeezed into a bustier, pushing her voluminous breasts up. Her dark hair framed her powdered sallow face in tiny curls, and her vermillion lipstick had filled the cracks on her lips. She smiled, revealing an assortment of greying teeth, and spoke French with a Greek accent as she invited them in. "Welcome to the House with the Piano, gentlemen." An immense chandelier hung in the center of the waiting room from a very high, ornate ceiling. Women in various stages of undress were sitting with customers on sofas and armchairs; a fragile-looking man wearing glasses played popular tunes on the piano in one corner.

Antoni whispered something to the old lady, who nodded and went off in a hurry.

He turned to Manolis. "Told her we wanted Despina. I go first, then you."

Manolis nodded and he sat down, observing the people in the room.

Antoni was right. The men were all middle-aged and older, dressed in expensive suits, which had by now rumpled. They were all familiar with each other and the women entertaining them. Despina appeared in the doorway. She was a petite woman wearing a pink satin negligee, with a long pearl necklace that went down to her navel. She had white silk stockings and high heels that showed off shapely calves. A small mouth, painted pink, seemed to be glued into a pout and her large hazel eyes were hidden by strands of chestnut hair. The two men sat gaping until, with a bored expression, she summoned, "Antoni, you first?" Antoni rose and followed her up the stairs, twisting his cap in his hands.

Manolis felt trapped in a surreal dream as he looked around. Here he was, across town in a bordello, half drunk, accompanied by a man whom only a few hours ago he'd suspected of betrayal and pondered on how to dispose of. Now he was sitting among half-naked men in various degrees of stupor, waiting for his turn to have the same woman as this man he hardly even knew, simply for not wanting to lose sight of him. She was quite beautiful, but still . . . He looked at his pants, feeling some awakening. The old woman approached and asked him to pay now if he did not mind. He took out his wallet and paid, as Antoni came down the stairs with a light step.

"That was fast," mocked Manolis. He arose, his heart sinking as he climbed the stairs. Being with a prostitute was a feeling akin to wearing someone else's underwear. He opened the door to the room where she was waiting. She removed the silk gown mechanically, exposing her breasts and pointed to the sink. As he washed himself under her scrutiny, he realized he had never quite enjoyed sexual encounters in his life, since they had only been with prostitutes. He wondered about Elena and how she would feel in a naked embrace. How it would feel to love a woman's body as opposed to using it. He imagined falling asleep inhaling Elena's perfumed locks, cupping her warm breasts in his palms. Marriage, he gathered from his conversations with friends, did not seem to provide sexual bliss at all. Girls who had never seen a man naked until their wedding night, ran back to their mothers' homes shrieking when presented with the dark, fleshy triumvirate hanging between hairy legs. Once tamed, they would obediently suffer the sight of this abomination and do their conjugal duty to procreate. Either way, it seemed to him, sex was less a pleasure than a necessity. You either got the devastated prostitute or the fearful wife. He lay down with Despina absentmindedly and went through the motions until the thoughts simply ceased rolling in his mind, leaving him alone with his body and the sight of hers moving under his weight.

He pulled up his trousers and went downstairs, having thanked her politely, unable to suppress a feeling of embarrassment when his eyes fleetingly met hers. Antoni was sitting on the sofa, eyes closed. He looked even younger in his slumber. Manolis shook him lightly to wake him up.

"Let's take a carriage, I'll let you off wherever you want," Manolis said. They got out into the street and hailed the first carriage. This way, Manolis made sure he knew where Antoni lived. Then he went home exhausted. He was satisfied that Antoni would go nowhere the remaning night. Manolis would have him followed the next day, just to be on the safe side, but he felt relieved not to have discovered anything suspicious. When he got into his house he crossed himself. He was not particularly religious or inclined to perform such gestures, but he felt he had somehow been protected from committing a heinous act whose consequences would have haunted him the rest of his life. He was grateful.

What he did not realize was that Antoni had been visiting Despina for some time, saving all his money for a moment with her every week. He started passing information to her innocently, mostly to give himself an air of importance, to make up for his youthful awkwardness in her jaded eyes. He never suspected she might pass it on to someone else. Antoni never discovered his own betrayal. Neither did Manolis who, after all the men had been under surveillance for a few days, concluded that the information could not have leaked from his own team.

A Picnic

SPRING CAME A FEW WEEKS LATER. Manolis offered to take everyone to a picnic in late February when the almond trees had bloomed. A wealthy and grateful patient had lent him his car for the day. He was eager to try it out. Curious how he ended up with a camera for delivering babies, and now this car for saving a rich man from undelivered farts, mused Elena out loud. Unusual favours for merely doing his job, added Polycarp, loosening his tie.

"What are you, Bolsheviks?" Manolis laughed nervously as he helped Elena carry her easel and painting gear into the car.

"You save the poor, the needy, the mutilated. Not just the rich and flatulent."

"Look, if it bothers you so much, we don't need to go."

"Never mind, that's not the point," she snapped.

Marie was stuffing a tablecloth into Elena's hand, pinching her wrist at the same time. Her not so subtle way of telling her daughter to be quiet and behave. She placed a wide-brimmed hat, overflowing with ribbons, on Elena's head, made by their father almost half a century ago, when Marie was a young bride. Elena had to wear it lest she hurt her mother's feelings.

Polycarp and Niko sat in the back seat while Elena sat beside Manolis. Everyone had to wear hats, Manolis insisted, because the speed of a car was dangerous for one's head. Polycarp threw his cap down as the car took off. It was one of the most exhilarating experiences of Niko's young life, to feel the wind whip his face and to watch the world speed by. The olive tree with the swollen joints of an old woman, fragments of white cloth tied to its branches like captive doves fluttering their wings in anticipation of a flight that never takes place. The old peasant hunchback leading a docile donkey swaying under his weight. A triangular formation of swallows in flight like a cloud above a field. Turquoise waves throwing shreds of dark green algae and spuds over wet rocks to gather them all back in retreat. A fisherman by the side of the road, standing behind a red wooden platter, pouring water on his catch of çipura and levrek, the silver scales of their bodies gleaming with each contortion of voiceless agony. He would remember these things.

They arrived in Narlıdere about an hour later.

Pomegranate and citrus trees covered the entire stretch from the mountains to the sea like a fragrant carpet. Venturing into a dusty path, they discovered a clearing where Elena could set up her easel. By the time Manolis stopped the car they were covered with terracota dust and bits of gravel.

Elena organized her tubes and brushes while the men emptied the car and prepared the picnic. Niko was already catching grasshoppers and stuffing them into a jar, hoping to exchange them later for John Krammer's German pen, which had a little destroyer in its aquatic chamber. John Krammer had been torturing Niko for weeks, tilting the pen back and forth in Frere André's grammar class. Niko had already offered him his only ink bottle, a dried up dung beetle, and uncle Polycarp's miniature French-Latin dictionary, which he had had to sneak out of his room on one of Ayşe's Wednesday visits. The snob would just shake his head no, tilting his trophy up and down. The grasshoppers would be Niko's last offer of exchange.

Elena had started sketching, and Polycarp, looking over her shoulder, said, "Trees . . . I suppose that's safe. More trees. A brook, a house in the distance. Maybe you can sell it for a good price."

"What are you suggesting?"

"How about the citrus trees in the background and Manolis in the foreground, next to the car. Smoking a cigar, in fact . . . Then he can hang this one in his clinic next to *Venice,* right Mano?" He winked at Niko.

Manolis was looking for something in the trunk. "Eh?"

"I said we should play a game of tavla."

Mano had a better idea. He brought out a camera to take a picture. He snapped one of Elena by her easel. And a family portrait of Elena, Pol, and Niko around the tablecloth. He painstakingly organized the composition "to make sure it will look entirely respectable to the eyes of posterity," he elaborated. Niko didn't know the word, so Manolis explained that one or even two hundred years from now, the great-grand children would know how they looked even though their kokalakia* would be very white indeed in their graves. Pol then mused whether two hundred years from now they would even care to know how ancestors looked. Niko reflected that it might be good to have pictures of their kokalakia taken as well, so the great-grand children would know which face went with which skull. Elena guffawed and hit him on the back of the head. Manolis got impatient and shouted, "Bre Syopi!" Shut Up. As he hid under the black curtain to finally freeze the moment, Pol picked up Elena's old fashioned hat, slapped it on his head and stood up shouting, "To the eye of my posterior!" It was too late. Manolis captured the moment with Pol's arms flying about in a grandiose gesture, the gauzy ribboned hat on his head and the rest of the family looking up at him, their faces contorted into different shapes of hilarity. There was a jar of grasshoppers on the ground that looked like it had dropped out of Niko's fingers, which were still stretched open as his head rolled back in laughter.

After lunch they tidied up and got in the car. Manolis drove very quietly. Pol sang a Greek song about Venizelos, the Greek prime

* little bones

minister whose dream was to recapture what once had belonged to
Byzantium. He had coined the term "Megaloidea," inflaming the
Greeks with a zeal to fight a war against the now defunct Ottoman Empire, with British support. The song was popular among
Greek schoolchildren in Smyrna. Pol kept inserting scatological
attributes to Venizelos in the song, making Niko laugh. Manolis
twitched uncomfortably and finally interjected flatly, "Venizelos is
a hero to some people."

Polycarp mused, "Wanting to tear a piece of flesh out of a carcass is hardly heroic."

Manolis smiled. "Anyone who is able to galvanize a nation
behind a grand idea is a hero."

"He might also be a clever opportunist who observes the political turmoil in Greece and thinks, 'Here's my golden opportunity!
Let's take out our ancient grudge against the Turks whose empire
dominated us for hundreds of years, now that it's safely defunct,
and let's build me a political career.' However, I am not an expert in
politics as you obviously are. By the way, this grudge, I'll have you
know, is much older than the Turks. The feud goes back thousands
of years, and way before Christ. Remember Troy?"

"Who cares about Troy? We're talking about right now and
Venizelos."

"Think about this: if the Ottomans hadn't let the domin-
ions govern themselves, you and your hero would be chanting
Allahüekber facing Mecca, fully circumcised. And second of all,
Venizelos would not be able to do much without the British, who
want Anatolia, all of it. But their public is fed up and tired. They
don't want another Gallipoli. Who's to do the dirty work? Not to
mention their culturally senile adoration of everything Greek, so
it's a perfect match!"

"What now? Are you going to put down Greek civilization
next?"

"Of course not. But how many know Greek from Anatolian or
Macedonian? To them, it is all one big basket of figs. They think

Trojans were Greeks. They think Alexander was Greek. Some wear turbans and silk shalvars to look exotically Ottoman while having their five o'clock tea, others live on the Aegean islands to write poetry and sell guns to Greek peasants in exchange for inhaling goat manure . . . This subject is boring me."

Manolis recited,

> "Awake! (not Greece—she is awake!)
> Awake, my spirit! Think through whom
> . Thy life-blood tracks its parent lake,
> And then strike home!

"I think it's beautiful."

Niko asked, "What is that?"

Polycarp responded, "Lord Byron. And if you listen to it carefully, you may hear the voice of a man with an urgent . . . Would you recite it for the boy again, Doctor?"

"I will not be party to such vulgarity!" snapped Manolis.

"Mano, Mano . . . Where is your sense of humour? This is not vulgarity. Is silliness not at all allowed in this car?"

Mano's voice cracked, "You take everything I hold dear and you just . . . you just . . . " He was tapping the steering wheel, "and you turn it to shit!" Jets of spit sprayed his fingers. "I'm sorry!" he apologized, wiping one hand with the other. Polycarp's bittersweet smile was barely noticeable. "Now, now . . . I'm supposed to be the madman around here. Such passion, my friend . . . What for? Are you going to change the world?"

"Maybe not the world, Polycarp . . . Maybe not the whole world, but my world, yes! Is it wrong to want to preserve my small world, my parents' vineyard, my Greekness in a sea of Turks? Tell me, is it? If Venizelos promises me that, I'm all for him!"

He took out his handkerchief from his pocket and wiped the nape of his neck and the beads of sweat on his upper lip.

"What do you think is going to happen to your beloved Smyrna now?"

No one responded.

When they arrived home, Manolis politely unloaded Elena's things, said goodnight to Marie and disappeared. Polycarp remained pensive the rest of the evening.

The Occupation

THE NEIGHBOUR FROM ACROSS the street had a shiny gramophone with a golden lily-shaped cone. It was the only gramophone in Aya Katerina. Every evening he could be seen sitting in profile by his window at what perhaps was his desk, on the second floor of his house, with the insturments in full view. He would pace, sit down, stare at the ceiling where the gramophone played. Operaphobes complained. Others gathered discreetly outside his house on warm nights to chat, nibble on sunflower seeds, and hear Caruso's voice pipe out from his window and into the narrow street of the quarter. Poplar trees rustled to the mellow rush of the imbat blowing in from the Aegean.

His name was Nazım, but everyone called him Karuso Efendi or Karuso Bey. Toothless Ahmet, even. "Günaydın Karasu˙ Efendi!" he'd say, mispronouncing, pulling Five Legs along. Eventually the misnomer Karasu became part of Nazım's name.

Elena knew that he was a journalist. "For an obscure communist newspaper, no doubt!" added Manolis. "So?" retorted Polycarp. Manolis asked, his eyes fixed on Elena, "Who's ever read anything he's written?" Elena shrugged and kept looking at Nazım Karasu's window.

There were rumours. Some linked him with Despina the famed prostitute, some linked him with Van der Meer, the Dutch ship-

˙Blackwater

ping magnate, and others pointed to his affiliation with the Bolsheviks. His father had been a general in the Sultan's army and
Nazım Karasu was indeed a journalist who wrote for an obscure
communist paper. He was educated, in Geneva, and spoke excellent French. They said he had gotten his revolutionary ideas while
studying in Switzerland, but was expelled from the exclusive
boys' school for insulting a history teacher who had asserted that
the Ottomans were barbarians and their empire a carbuncle that
needed to be excised from the bums of Europe for civilized ideals
to prevail. According to Abdulselâm, the grocer who had heard
the story from the proud general himself, Nazım had responded by
defecating on the teacher's lecture notes.

By 1919, everyone in Smyrna lived with the near certainty that
the Greeks would invade Anatolia. The Great War had ripped the
Ottoman Empire to shreds; the vultures were circling in, choos-
ing the prime cuts. The Sultan was selling to the highest bidder,
so to speak. Border guards were instructed to turn a blind eye to
arms shipments destined for local Greeks. The British were ready
to pounce on Constantinople, and they did. On May 19, 1919 the
news came that Constantinople was under British protection and
the Sultan had fled the country with his wives and children.

The local Greeks in Aya Katerina, noted Marie, had been burying their smuggled arms in their backyards. She saw many of them
at night digging holes, and they didn't all have dead dogs that
needed burying. The Orthodox Greek church, it was rumoured,
was distributing the weapons. Everybody knew what was coming.
Or thought they did.

The day the Greeks invaded Smyrna, Polycarp disappeared. He
had left the house the night before while the family slept so that no
one knew he was missing until much later. He had been drawing
maps of Izmir's various quarters for weeks. When Niko asked what
the maps were for, he responded with a conspiratorial nod that he
had decided finally to give away Smyrna. Why, asked Niko.

"Because if I don't, they'll rob and ruin it."

It was his grandmother who discovered that Polycarp was gone. Her cries echoed through the house. "Polycarp is gone! Wake up! Wake up, Elena, Polycarp is gone! Mother of God help me find him . . . Saint Antoine help me find my son . . . "

They all ran out into the street when they heard the sound of cheerful band music outside. It was coming from the port. They hastened towards it. British and Greek flags were flying in all sizes. Greek schoolchildren, their hair combed with lemon juice for extra shine, were marching in pairs toward the Quay. There were crowds everywhere—walking, standing, pushing. Niko and the rest had to push their way through the dense crowds. His grandmother's dishevelled white hair was like cotton plucked out of a bag. Her eyes darting in their dark sockets searching for her son in the crowds. Her lips moved in prayer and her hands were outstretched to open the way. No one saw them. All eyes were fixed towards the Greek warships docked in Pasaport. Orthodox priests in long black robes and tall headgear walked alongside the Greek soldiers.

"Patriarch Chrisostomos is there, see?" "Ahh yes." "Who?" "Chrisostomos." Fingers pointing vaguely. People observing the parade from open windows. French horns, trumpets, drums. Niko's hand squeezed into his aunt's. No sight of Polycarp. They were pushed along, compressed together, knuckles hurting. The Evzon soldiers with their pompoms and white skirts marched to the beat of the drums. The sound of a gun firing. An abrupt POCKK echoing back and forth among the buildings. Then another. A collective sigh. A woman's voice shrieking, "They're shooting at the soldiers. Move back!" A wave of panic, the crowds attempting to disperse, but moving slowly, trapped by its own mass.

Greek soldiers were moving into the crowd, bayonets raised. From the corner of an eye, Niko saw a dead soldier sprawled on the pavement, blood leaking in rivulets around his head. Elena covered Niko's eyes with her jacket. "Don't look anywhere," she kept whispering. "Mama, shield the boy." Niko was between grandmother and aunt, their arms shielding him. The crowd started thinning out, retreating into the side streets. Soldiers running. Screams. A dead man, his fez, just tumbled off his head, still rolling on the sidewalk. Aunt's jacket covering Niko's eyes. Walking hurriedly, trying not to attract attention. Grandmother sobbing, her chin tucked into her neck. As they advanced, they saw more and more dead people on the street. Some of them women. A small child. Praying praying praying not to be noticed by someone with a gun or a bayonet. Sweat running down the side of Niko's face into his ears. In his head, the images of death. Fear, of being recognized as a Turk, a Greek, an Armenian, a child. Someone unwanted and expendable. Like his father. Having the wrong name or the wrong face. Wearing the wrong hat or facial expression. A fog of dust everywhere, raised by the running feet.

They returned to their street, muted sounds of gunshots, screams, running feet echoing in their ears. At the corner, a crowd of people were gathered around the house of Emine Hanım and her husband Vehbi Bey, also known as Köfte. Two Greek levendis with thick black moustaches, armed with swords, were dragging the old couple by their hair out of their house, shouting obscenities. The old man's face was bloodied and swollen. The old lady was begging for mercy for the love of God. A levendi kicked her in the leg, called her a dirty Turkish bitch, and threatened to slit her throat. The neighbours stood staring as if in a trance. Kiryo Papayannis, who lived across the street, appeared in his doorway with his rifle pointed in their direction and walked slowly out into the street. Heads turned. His voice boomed out in Greek. "You are the dogs, pezevengithi! Get your filthy hands off before I send you both to hell. Move, or I shoot your legs off!"

His face had turned crimson. He approached the levendis without hesitation, his hunting rifle at one of the men's crotch. He was a stocky man, Kiryo Papayannis. His abdomen barreled out in front of him, framed by suspenders. His anger made him look taller, raising his leonine grey mane around his head. The crowd had parted to let him through. The levendis dropped the old couple and fled. "Coproskili!" he boomed after them. Slowly the neighbours came to life. Two women helped the old couple get back into their house. Kiryo Papayannis was not moving from his place. He kept looking in the direction of the fleeing thugs, his gun still raised. After what seemed like a very long time, he spat on the ground at the feet of the remaining neighbours, turned around, and walked back to his house, slamming the door behind him.

Niko recalled the cinnamon candies Emine Hanım used to give him whenever his grandmother sent him to her house for a sprig of parsley, a lemon, or an egg. They were pyramid-shaped, bright red, and hard, like precious stones. They slowly melted in the cheeks making them protrude in fleshy cones while stinging the tongue. He kept thinking about the candy, it's shape, texture, and taste to blanket the vision of the old lady whose worn slipper had flown out onto the pavement when she received a kick on her thigh.

Grandmother bolted the door. She called for Polycarp but there was no answer. She sat on the floor and stared at the tiles as though trying to make sense of the geometry. She instructed everyone to close the shutters and go upstairs, after asking Elena to bring her grandfather's hunting rifle. Niko lay in his darkened room wondering how many coffins and nails would be needed to tear the glaring eyes of the dead from his beloved Smyrna-blue skies. His teeth started chattering uncontrollably. He expected the two Greek thugs to come back, break the door down, drag them all out by the hair. Nowhere to hide. No secret passages in basements. They would find him under the bed, the orphan whose father was an Ottoman soldier, a potential enemy of the Greeks. "Slit his throat." A nine-year-old bleeding to death.

A few hours must have passed. The afternoon shadows were creeping up from the tree branches onto the verandah in elongated dark slivers, stretching and shrinking with the breeze. A knock on the door was followed by another, and another. Niko ran down the stairs. His grandmother had fallen asleep in a heap on the floor by the door.

She slowly opened her eyes and asked Niko, whose legs were shaking with terror, to help her rise.

"Yes?" she asked tremulously through the door.

"Nazım, your neighbour. May I speak with you? I mean no harm. I'm a friend."

She opened the door just a crack to see who was there, pointing her rifle. "What about?"

"Polycarp . . . "

She opened the door wide. "Where is he?"

"In my house. I found him unconscious in an alley in Kemeraltı. He isn't hurt. Feverish, probably. He told me his name and where he lived."

Marie hurried out of the house, nudging Nazım's elbow to take him to her son. She told Niko to wake his aunt and bolt the door.

Polycarp lay in bed delirious for weeks. Manolis put leeches on his back to take away his chill. Marie prepared herbal remedies to calm his nerves with Emine Hanım's recipes. Nazım politely came to inquire about Polycarp's health every evening. He would briefly stand at the doorway and speak with Elena, refusing her invitations to come in for tea, saying he had much to do.

Finally one day he walked in, took off his shoes in the doorway, and entered the house, stepping gingerly on the kilims. He tiptoed his way into the living room to the sofa where Polycarp lay reading, propped up by pillows. Elena, Marie, and Niko were sitting on the couch side by side observing the newcomer. It was hard to tell how old he was. His greenish eyes seemed to penetrate everything upon which they fixed. He had recently shaved off his moustache. Elena could not keep her eyes off his hands. He had long bony fingers that made him look fragile and masculine at the same time. She rose, offering tea. His eyes smiled as he nodded, and the long bony fingers of both hands came together, locking loosely. He asked Polycarp how he was feeling. Marie interjected quickly, thanking him for finding her son. In the midst of this tragedy, she had lost hope of finding him alive, she explained. They exchanged news of the day. Nazım did most of the talking. He mentioned the hangings in front of city hall that happened on a daily basis now. They hanged the presumed insurgents after interrogation, which consisted of beatings and torture and resulted in confessions. The suspects were then quickly tried, found guilty, and executed in the plaza for all to see. The day before, he had witnessed the hanging of an old Jewish cloth merchant.

"He was a frail man, old enough to be my father," Nazım said. "His wife and children were sobbing and pleading in the crowd. A soldier walked up to the wife and told her to end the spectacle or her son would also be hanged."

Their eyes grew round in horror as he recounted what he had seen.

"Better to stay indoors for a while. Bolt the doors and shutters. The air is fresher inside this house than outdoors, anyway. They have to remove all the dead lying in the streets and floating in the sea. It's going to take time. If you must go out, make sure you don't go far and look down when you walk."

Niko's hands started shaking.

Nazım, noticing this, quickly apologized. "I'm sorry. I shouldn't have told you. It is just too horrible." He shook his head. "I haven't slept in days."

Elena came back with cups of tea. As they drank the weak sugarless tea she stared at his hands, unable to figure out why she was so moved by them. He caught her stare as he raised his cup to his lips and looked straight into her eyes. Elena pulled her gaze away with difficulty, wondering if anyone had noticed the exchange. There was nothing subtle about it. He finished his tea quickly and rose, asking them to let him know if they needed anything, as he did not judge it safe for children and women to go outdoors for the next few weeks. He shook hands with everyone. Elena was the last. Her hand lingered in his a while then he was gone.

Weeks later, when Polycarp was able to make some sense of

what had happened to him that day, he told Niko, in secret, that Nazım had been running down the street where he sat huddled in the doorway of a closed store with his bed covers around him. Nazım looked terrified, he was stuffing his handgun into his belt when he saw Polycarp and recognized him.

"They're looking for me," he whispered.

Pol hid him under his covers. Soon after, Greek soldiers came running down the street, bayonets raised, looking for him. They didn't pay attention to Polycarp and his bundles, taking him for a beggar.

Once they disappeared from sight, Polycarp and Nazım made their way back to Aya Katerina and hid in Nazım's house. Polycarp thought he must have passed out because his memory of the event stopped there. He made Niko promise to tell no one. Niko nodded, feeling unsure whether this was one of his uncle's delusions or the truth.

Spinoza

THEY VENTURED OUTSIDE, RELUCTANTLY at first. With each outing they discovered that their world had vanished a little more, to be replaced by another. Familiar faces looked foreign. Eyebrows walked the streets in burly knots, eyes were fixed on cobblestones. Hands clutched canes when they did not hide in pockets. Feet shuffled underneath limp trousers. Fezzes stayed away. The jeweller no longer sat on a stool by his shop counting his worry beads. His windows had been smashed, the door was boarded. Adem Bey was not in his butcher shop. They heard from the Greek baker that he had been strangled to death and strung on a brass hook along with his helper. His Cretan origins and his wife's Greek name did nothing to change his fate. Fotini, his wife, had shrunk to the size of a pencil.

The school year remained unfinished when summer came. The French friars came to the students' homes and offered to continue classes through the summer months. Unfortunately for Niko, his grandmother agreed to send him, so that he sat at his desk in his black uniform with a handful of other students in the sweltering summer heat. The Patterson twins, Krammer, and a few others were there, but Aziz was gone. Niko heard that his family had moved to Ankara, abandoning their house to looters. The streets were adorned with Greek flags. Soldiers were on patrol. The friars, to cheer the boys up, decided to create a school band with drums, flutes, trumpets, and trombones. Niko played the piccolo. Frère Felix taught them to play Bizet's *Carmen*, and soon they were parading through the streets of Izmir playing *Carmen* and getting smacked by his enormous hands whenever they missed a beat. Niko was at the front, walking ahead of the others due to his small frame, palms sweating at the thought of receiving Cher Frère's paw on his bottom. Like underfed crows on a clothesline they lined up at the Quay to give concerts, and get sprayed by the afternoon waves. Polycarp came to watch. Then he would take Niko by the hand and walk him home absentmindedly. At first, Niko rejoiced, thinking his uncle had come to listen to him play. As his share of Frère Felix's smacks diminished, his musical pride rose, to the point where he imagined the familiar old ladies lined up on the other side of the Quay, also dressed in black, whispering to each other, "Jacob's Orphan has exceptional musical talent, poor little fellow . . . " He soon realized that the old ladies came merely for the breeze, they were there whether the boys came to play or not. And he began to suspect that his uncle had another motive for coming to listen to him. He was doing his best to avoid Manolis.

On their way home one afternoon, Polycarp looked at his nephew and nodded with a conspiratorial wink, as if emphasizing his point in the middle of a sentence, but there had been no conversation at all.

He then said, "Let's take a detour today. I think Manolis is still visiting. He's all cheery lately, whistling in and out of our house."

He looked at Niko and shrugged. "I can't stand it?" It was not a question, but it sounded like one. The boy nodded, unable to think of something to say.

"He gives your aunt these syrupy looks that churn my stomach. When he's tired of spreading sticky looks, I have to play the blasted tavla with him. I despise the game! You throw the dice and count. Throw the dice and count. On top of that, I win every time, but he's the one whistling. I don't understand how they made him a doctor, if he can't even win one miserable game of tavla against a madman. Eh? His dog's farts would awaken the dead. Some hunter he is. What does he feed the brute anyway?"

Abruptly, he looked up at the sky. "Look up! What's that?"

"A locomotive?" Niko attempted. An old game they played.

"Yes . . . yes . . . That must be it."

He sighed. "How many licks did you get from Frère Felix today?"

"None!" Niko beamed.

"That's good," Polycarp chuckled and continued as though he hadn't interrupted himself, "I think he had something to do with the occupation."

"Frère Felix?"

"Manolis, dummy! Manolis had something to do with the occupation. In the evenings, he's been running to these political meetings . . . I'm sure he goes to meetings, where else? He's not clever enough to find a bordello by himself, is he? If only someone would show him one. It might help him lose those saccharine smiles cramping his face like rigor mortis and do everyone a favour."

He sighed, while Niko laughed and blushed. He wasn't sure what bordellos were, but had a vague idea they were places where women sat in underclothes and smoked cigarettes while men gaped. His uncle's monologue was becoming completely unintelligible to him.

"Mark my words, Niko. Manolis is going to become some big shot. Some mayor or something flashy in Greek Smyrna. He's been praying for this to happen for years, I bet. I watched him. I watched him for months before the occupation. He always left the house at the same time in the evening. Sometimes men would come and get him. He never took his bag, so he wasn't making house calls. What was he doing."

This one was a question but sounded like a firm statement. Niko didn't need to answer it.

"I don't buy for a minute that he got that car for our picnic in return for curing a rich old man. Rich men don't remain grateful long enough to remember such promises. The car was for something else. And then he will want to marry Elena. Your grandmother is already getting fluffy in the head, singing silly songs. Mind you, the only dowry your aunt can manage are her—"

"Paintings!" Niko finished. It seemed like an obvious conclusion.

"Right," Polycarp seemed amused. "Let's go to the pet shop."

"Eh?"

"I'll get us a parakeet. Would you like a green one that talks? Or would you rather have a fish?"

They turned into a side street.

"Look at that man!" Polycarp whispered urgently, nodding towards a middle-aged man walking ahead of them.

Niko turned and looked at his uncle questioningly.

"Don't you see something strange?"

He was a heavy-set man with a fashionably twirly moustache, dressed in a gray suit.

"Doesn't the moustache look false? Like a disguise? And the suit . . . " He went on hurriedly, "It hangs off his ass as if it belonged to someone bigger."

"You think he's from a circus?" Niko asked, hopeful.

"I just think he is not the man he appears to be. Maybe a spy. But whose spy? Who does he work for . . . "

To Niko, he looked like anybody's overworked father.

"Everyone you encounter in these streets nowadays is either a revolutionary or an informer."

"Wait here." Polycarp hurried towards the man and asked for the time. The man stopped and took out his pocket watch. Just as he was about to tell the time, Niko overheard his uncle say, "Had soup for lunch, didn't you? Wait, there's a noodle here." With this, he gave a slight tug to the man's brown moustache, which was artfully curled up like the handles of violins. The man practically jumped, covering his mouth with one hand. "Sir, I beg your pardon! What do you think . . . ?" He raised his cane with the other hand to fend off another possible attack.

Polycarp apologized profusely, looked at his hands pretending to search for the offensive noodle, took a bow and ran straight into the dingy pet store. Niko was ready for a green parakeet. There were only a couple of yellow canaries, some anemic goldfish in a blurry tank, and a puppy.

His uncle, sensing Niko's preference for the puppy, warned, "These grow and become like Katzathoro. Besides, they eat real food and we don't have any. I just have enough money for a bird or a fish, so decide."

They returned home with a yellow canary in a cage.

Marie greeted them at the door. Crossing herself repeatedly she kept mumbling, "Dear God, what did I do to you that you treat me this way? You don't think it enough that I must feed and clothe these people and you send me a bird too?"

Then she pointed her finger at Niko. "YOU will clean the cage. If I ever find droppings ANYWHERE in this house, YOU will be in big trouble."

There was no point in arguing it was Uncle Pol's idea. He had many ideas; this couldn't be helped. It was an unspoken rule in the house that whoever happened to be with Pol when he got an idea was responsible for its consequences.

Spinoza became Niko's daily ration of delight in a world that appeared greyer with every passing day. He sang. He ate seeds from their palms. They taught him to leave his cage and reenter it. He took to perching on Polycarp's shoulder without flying away, even when they left a window open. Even Marie seemed to be charmed by the yellow bird and cleaned up the cage while talking to it.

Since the occupation, she had avoided going to the market, so as not to be reminded of Butcher Adem's fate. She had known him all his life. From the time he was a young man with carrot hair, working in his father's store until he took over the business. Everyday she went down to the marketplace, and everyday she walked into his store to greet him. Whenever she went into Niko's room to dust the furniture, she would sit on the boy's bed and gaze at Adem's portrait on the wall, cross herself, and weep. One day Niko found her sobbing on her knees, leaning on his bed. She was the picture of devastation. He kneeled next to her and caressed the strands of white hair on top of her head. He rubbed her back, not knowing how to help.

"We've lost your father . . . your uncle's mind . . . our friends . . . our Smyrna . . . It's all gone. I could not spare you any of this," she managed in between sobs. He held her in his arms swaying back and forth.

"We are all orphans, Grandma," he whispered.

Later, after she had calmed down, he sat at his desk, took out his history book, and opened it to the designated page. The words were a blurr. Who were the orphan-makers, he wondered. Everyday men, were they? Yesterday they went out to buy bread, or played with their children, and today, away from their own lives, they saw it fit to hang, rape, pillage, and ruin. They were pious, surely, wherever their lives awaited them, untouched. But they could be monsters elsewhere. He shuddered. History was actually about the making of orphans, bread lines and hunger, poverty and the smell of death. It was about this, here. Grown men in uniforms waving banners over children's putrefied flesh and heartaches. He was going to tell Frère Felix his books were wrong. Written by liars. He shut the book in disgust and stuffed it back into his school bag.

Cordelio

A FEW WEEKS LATER, Elena finished *Peasant Banquet*. She called Polycarp to the attic to receive his opinion. When he reached the top of the stairs, Brueghel's *Banquet* stood there, in all its height. Polycarp's jaw dropped, he was speechless. He moved closer and then back, shaking his head.

"This is the real thing," he whispered. "How did you do it?" His eyes lit up. "You've put us all there! The lady with the bonnet is Mama. I'm the musician over there and Jacob is the bearded landowner. Niko is the one pouring water from a jug . . . "

Elena smiled, pleased that her brother had so quickly noticed the alterations. She meant them to be imperceptible. If Van der Meer noticed them, she would explain that it would be dishonest for her to make a carbon copy; for that, he had his reproductions. Satisfied that she could work on it no longer, she packed the painting and asked for a horse carriage to pick her up at her house. She would deliver it directly to his mansion in Cordelio, to avoid passing by the scene of the massacre.

It was late summer, when the world takes on the golden hue of scorched grass and shrubs in Smyrna. August being jellyfish season, she could see hundreds of large, soft blue domes bobbing in and out of the water, riding the waves lazily in the shallow parts of the bay. Men and women strolled with damp half moons of sweat under the arms and full moons on their backsides. This was a challenging season for Polycarp, mused Elena, with the orders for wide-brimmed hats coming in dozens. He could not afford mishaps with his scissors, his bucket hat substitutes were now received by customers with scowls and threats to take their business elsewhere. To avoid accidents, Niko spent his free time at the shop cutting the cardboard and cloth into wide brims, which his uncle would then press into shape. Elena had not been to the store in a while. In fact, she had not been anywhere but to the attic. Being out in the sun, watching the world go by from a horse carriage felt good. She adjusted her hat to avoid the glare in her eyes. Cordelio's villas and mansions soon appeared on the right side of the road. The left side was flanked by a sea wall. Shrieks of joy echoed in the air, as children splashed around in the calm sea.

The horses pulling the carriage also wore wide-brimmed straw hats against sunstrokes. Their muscles moved under their skin like furry animals. The driver, also in a straw hat, was looking from side to side, holding the reins loosely, letting his horses lead the way.

The mansion was towards the edge of Cordelio where it stood alone, surrounded by marshes and fields. High walls encircled about two-thirds of the immense property, the rest was surrounded by a wire fence all the way to the sea. Of the extended property only the beach was visible from outside. The house was built in the style of an eighteenth-century French chateau, though smaller. It had a yellow facade. Arriving at the wrought-iron gate, the driver got off the carriage and rang the bell. The guard appeared from the side and, inquiring about their purpose, let them in. The carriage entered the unpaved driveway up to the house and she alighted. She walked to the door, knocked and waited, adjusting her hat and gloves. A housekeeper in a white apron and bonnet opened the door and let her in.

Elena waited in an antechamber until the housekeeper, having announced her, came back in and took her hat. She led Elena to the library, to meet Van der Meer. Elena walked into the middle of the room holding her wrapped canvas in front of her. When she lowered it the person standing in front of her was not Van der Meer but Nazım, the journalist. She blinked and looked around, confused. Van der Meer was sitting farther off to the side; he rose and came towards her, his hand extended.

"Mademoiselle Devision, how do you do."

She shook hands automatically, still confused.

"Let me introduce you to my good friend Nazım Bey," Van der Meer raised a hand towards the journalist, whose eyes were latched onto hers and held them.

Nazım offered, "We have already met. How do you do?"

She averted her eyes and managed a faint smile. "Indeed, we have," she said, having recovered her composure a little. "But what a surprise!"

She looked around for a place to lean the canvas on.

"Please, please allow me," the host moved quickly to hold the painting and leaned it towards the wall. "Have a seat. Can I offer you tea?"

She asked for a cold glass of water instead, trying not to move her arms too much, wary of the sweat stains underneath.

They sat facing each other, with the covered painting behind them like a pupil standing in the corner of the classroom in a dunce hat. Van der Meer, sensing her discomfort, explained to Nazım that Ms Devision was a very talented painter and had graciously agreed to reproduce for him *Peasant Banquet* by Brueghel the Elder.

Nazım was amazed to find out that Elena was a painter, and not just the Levantine neighbour down the street. He nodded absently as he listened to Van der Meer reciting her praises, and his green eyes searched hers, the fingers in his long bony hands loosely together in front of him in a gesture she remembered vividly. She swallowed to push down her heart which had risen to her throat, searching for a calming phrase to plug into her mind. The long bony hands and the greenish eyes seemed everywhere. She refocused her sight on an absurd-looking porcelain figurine, a Madame Pompadour lookalike, standing proudly on a crocheted white doily. There was silence in the room. Both men were looking at her. She realized Van der Meer had stopped talking and was waiting for an answer.

"I'm sorry . . . I . . . this porcelain figurine . . . It looks like an antique . . . "

Van der Meer came to her rescue. "My mother used to collect them. They are everywhere in the house, lurking behind every door, causing the housekeeper great anxiety. I was asking if you minded my taking the wrappings off the canvas now. Nazım Bey is a good friend and I'm sure he is as eager as I am to see it."

She nodded, sank back into her chair. The tall man rose and went to the canvas, and unwrapped the coarse brown paper gently, letting it fall to the floor.

As the two men stood together watching the painting, their backs turned to her, she stood up and gingerly walked to the open window. A soft imbat breeze blew into the room, freshening the skin on her face and hands. She gazed at the sea swaying heavily, children bobbing up and down in it. A boxy governess was waving from the shore, telling them to get out of the water. Elena was hoping the two men would not say polite, meaningless things for her benefit. The governess was clapping her hands and waving frantically.

Van der Meer came to Elena and stood by the window, facing the sea, his eyes moist. "I do not know how to thank you for this," he said, then turned and kissed her hand. "You are indeed an excellent painter, Miss Devision. Merci." Elena looked quickly at him. "It is Brueghel who is the great painter. I have only copied him."

She looked back at the scene outside.

"Do not be so modest, Mademoiselle. Only a very talented painter could copy Brueghel so faithfully."

The governess was marching to the edge of the boardwalk, hoping to be seen by the children. There was fury in her gait. Elena smiled and thanked Van der Meer. She pulled away from the window, her mind still on the scene outside, and advanced towards the centre of the room. She picked up her purse and extended her hand to her host. Van der Meer asked her to follow him to his desk where he quickly opened a drawer and produced an envelope.

"For the next commission. Your choice."

She took the envelope and blurted, *"Dulle Griet . . .* I could copy *Dulle Griet."*

She had not planned on it.

He nodded. "I see . . . So be it."

"I already have the reproduction," she replied, as she endeavoured to stuff the envelope into her small purse, making a mental note to purchase a larger one, so she would not have to do this so ungracefully in the future. She extended her hand to Nazım, trying to avoid meeting his eyes, and mumbled something polite about the pleasure of seeing him again. He said he also had to leave, and he would be honoured to have the pleasure of her company.

They climbed into the carriage that was waiting in front of the mansion. Facing her, he was able to hold her gaze in his for the first few minutes of the trip, after which she turned away to look at the passing scenery. When she looked back at him, he caught her gaze again and she let him keep it. After a while, he looked down at his hands and away at the seashore. Neither of them made any effort to dissolve the uneasiness in small talk. He leaned his head back and closed his eyes so she could observe him freely. He half-opened his eyelids and found her gazing at his face. This made them both smile. The afternoon sun made him squint. She moved to one side of her seat and offered the other half to him to get out of the sun. As he sat beside her, the air moved, bringing a whiff of rose to his nose. He put his hands around his hat, on his knees. She had hers around her purse on her lap. She looked at the world go by and he looked the other way. His side had the view of the sea, so she turned to look there, her eyes occasionally moving down for a glimpse of his hands. He pretended to look in the other direction, where the houses were, in order to peek at the nape of her neck with its sweaty little curls smelling like roses. He forgot about the pretense of looking at pedestrians, freely relishing the sight of that downy nape with the little droplets of salty moisture, wanting to touch. It could not be helped. She turned and saw everything: his deliberate stare, the hand that left the bowler hat slowly and rose to the bottom of her hairline, brushing the back of her neck. She neither moved nor protested. The hair on her body stood on end, making her skin hurt. He rearranged a strand of hair that had come loose and put it behind her ear. She gave a shiver. He feared a slap in the face. It did not stop him. She remembered this was not proper etiquette, but she would bring it up later. Meanwhile she stared at his lips, noticing how plump and soft and close they seemed, and strangely familiar. He returned to his corner, looked away. "I'd been wanting to do this from the moment I first saw you," he said. Her eyes turned wide. "And I saw you long before you saw me."

"When was that?" she whispered.

"You were painting in your attic, late one night. I saw you staring out from your window, brush in hand, in a trance almost. You were staring in the direction of the sea. You stood there like a statue, not really seeing anything." The back of his fingers brushed her white knuckles clutching the purse.

"You looked frightening. For a moment I thought you were a ghost. Then you moved. You threw the brush where I could no longer see it and leaned the side of your forehead on the glass window. I could see your chest rising and falling. You were weeping." He put his hands back on his hat.

"From that night on, I watched you. I saw you running around the room with the boy, throwing pillows at each other and laughing. I thought he was your son . . . The Greek man stood under your window almost every night. He was watching you too."

"He was?"

He nodded.

"I watched you too," she replied. "You type and type late into the night, don't you? Are you a communist?"

"Is that what communists do? Type and type?"

"I heard you were. That's all."

"I'm a journalist."

She leaned back and closed her eyes. "I don't even know you."

He too leaned back. "Then we go back to watching each other secretly. You did not slap me just now when I touched you."

"I will, later."

"Come here."

"Where?"

"Here. I'll hold you until the carriage stops. Then you slap me or walk away . . . "

She hesitated.

He reached over and held her hand. "I'll just hold you for a while. You want it, too."

Shifting a few inches towards him was extremely awkward. She pulled back. He took her hand and kissed it, placing it gently on her lap.

"So be it. I shall go back to being your distant and devoted voyeur."

The trees lining the street were swaying this way and that, their rustling echoing the sea.

"The Greek man, who is he?"

"We grew up together. He is like a brother."

"I don't think he shares that feeling. Are you in a rush to get home?"

Elena looked at him, her eyebrows raised.

"We can get off this carriage and take a walk by the seaside, have lemonade. We can talk or sit quietly."

"You don't wear a fez . . . " she began, attempting to change the conversation.

"You don't like my hat?" He turned it around in the air, scrutinizing it. "Looks cheap, does it?"

"No, not at all. But . . . "

"But I'm not a Levantine, and so why am I wearing the wrong hat is that the question?"

"I didn't mean that. I was just . . . traditionally . . . "

"Traditionally, we would not be sharing a ride, sitting side by side. You would not be carrying paintings around the city by yourself, certainly not to the house of a bachelor, unaccompanied. In fact, you wouldn't be painting them at all. But if you insist on my being traditional, I'll wear a fez first thing tomorrow." He smiled gently.

"I've offended you."

"Not at all."

"Yes, I have. And I didn't mean to."

"No."

"Fine."

"Is there another part of my attire you prefer to discuss now?"

"I accept your offer."

Nazım looked at her, bemused.

"To walk around and so on . . . " She made a vague flourish with her hand.

He asked the driver to stop and helped her get down.

They walked along the seashore quietly, their clothes fluttering and the smell of algae seeping into their nostrils. She could see the sea bed, the rocks covered in green moss, and the brownish fish wiggling in and out of them. She selected a flat pebble and made it skip on the water, plip plip a few times and finally plop, relishing the sound of the stone being licked and finally swallowed. As it sank, concentric waves grew out of the liquid hole and disappeared in all the other motions of the sea. These were reassuring moments for her; doing things which elicited familiar results. The ride caused anxiety, whereas here in the open summer air things behaved predictably and this was fine. He was a thin man in a slightly crumpled suit, walking with his hands in his pockets, he appeared smaller now than a while ago. He took much less space and she was able to observe him from a distance.

He lingered behind as she walked a step ahead of him, watching her move like something with sails on, as the breeze filled her skirt before flapping it and retreating. She did not roll her hips but sauntered, swaying a little. One moment he thought she looked like a tea towel carried along by a whimsical wind, another moment she appeared to float on the pavement as if it were a liquid surface she had momentarily tamed. Yet she wore old shoes, the kind that buttoned up on the side, and her calves were strong. It was this strangeness about her that made him feel weak inside, he reflected. He wanted to protect this tea towel of a woman, and at the same time he knew this would, at best, be an imposition as she was also statuesque and seemed to require no protection.

They had walked a long while, she ahead of him, their silence interrupted occasionally by the noises of the skipping and sinking pebbles. Fishing boats were lined up in the horizon, waiting for the sun to go down, to lure unsuspecting fish into their nets. Camels went by, led by a donkey, their large bells chiming as they moved unhurriedly along the road. She asked him what he thought would happen now, with the occupation of Smyrna. Those who suffered the most were those who, as always, had no say—the hard-working poor, and they were the majority. He had no idea what would happen, but if he had his way, this majority would be organized into an army by an able leader. Mustafa Kemal was doing this precisely, he added quickly, to expel the European imperialists, and the Greek army, which he estimated was in chaos, to create a republic out of the Ottoman detritus. He hoped for a modern system based on enlightened ideals; the masses would need to be awakened out of their ignorant stupor and religious superstition. If he had his way, it would be a system that defended the poor and not only the rich and well-connected. He grew animated; his eyes seemed to focus everywhere and nowhere at once, as though a path had opened up in front of him and he was taking pains to determine its exact direction.

"So you are a Bolshevik, after all," smiled Elena.

"I am not," he asserted. "But I do sympathize with their desire to create an equitable society. How can one not dream of that? The struggle to create a classless society, a true democracy. How can one not aspire to it?"

Elena interjected, "You believe it is possible to achieve this by expelling the occupiers and imperialists from this land?"

"No," he corrected. "I simply do not believe this is possible while we remain in chains."

"What about Van der Meer?"

"He is an enlightened man and he will use his means to work for the common good."

"How did you two meet?"

"School in Switzerland. We were the only students from Izmir."

"Did you really get expelled from that school?"

"How would you know this?" He looked baffled.

"Abdulselâm the grocer. Your father told him a long time ago and he tells everyone. I think I know more about you than you do about me." Her step was energetic now and he took his hands out of his pockets trying to keep up with her.

"And you, what do you think will happen to Izmir?" He retaliated.

She looked back, her eyes mocking. "I expect you will save it, of course."

She threw one final stone and watched it skip before wiping her dusty hands on her dress. "But when you do, make sure to avoid another bloodbath." She walked towards the street in search of a carriage.

The treaty of Sèvres had been signed the same day. They had both read the papers that morning. It stipulated that Izmir would be administered by Greeks for the next five years, to be followed by a plebiscite to determine whether it would be Turkish or Greek. Thrace would be ceded to Greece, Constantinople would remain under Ottoman control, albeit with a garrison of former Entente powers. As they sat once again face to face in the cramped carriage, he commented on how the Treaty had come as an afterthought on the part of the Entente, after the invasion of Izmir by the Greeks. It was a rushed effort on the part of Lloyd George and his friend Venizelos to get there before the Italians, who had secretly been promised the spoils by the French. "They are all busy backstabbing each other, unaware that the invasion and the massacre that followed is fuel for Turkish nationalism. So in fact this is not such a bad thing, in the end . . . They all have their smug sights on that Ottoman ruin called the Sublime Porte in Istanbul, and do not even consider that Turkish nationalism may come and bite them from behind. They have not understood that the Turk is not an Ottoman in new clothes, but an entirely new entity inadvertently created by their Great War. You see? Let the Sultan sign the treaty and keep his throne. Do you notice the anger in people's eyes in the streets? The army gathering in the east, led by Kemal, is coming with sticks and stones, but no, no one can promise you there will not be a bloodbath. This is war, not a tea party. Your Rum friend, did he ever promise you there would be no bloodbath during the invasion?"

"What has he got to do with the invasion?" She frowned.

"He helped it happen. He worked for it. As if you did not know!" His face twisted involuntarily.

"Are you accusing him of plotting against the government merely because he is Rum?" She leaned forward, looking angry.

"I have been observing him. I know what he does. He gets his orders from Greece and belongs to an organization that helped bring about the invasion. I find it hard to believe you do not know this."

"How would I, and why should I believe you?"

"I haven't asked you to believe me. I also haven't concealed my beliefs and political inclinations. You can tell your friend about our conversation and I would be arrested and hanged tomorrow. I may be a fool for trusting you, a fool with a very short life ahead of him."

"Have you been watching me because of him? What are you going to do to him?"

"I have been watching you because you move me. The sight of you turns my legs to gruel. I don't know why. If I don't catch a glimpse of you one day, I feel restless. I watch you because I can't help it! When you sobbed that night, I wanted to be the window on which you rested your forehead. It is the most baffling sensation and I hate to feel it. I hate watching the Rum watching you. I started watching him because I had to, you understand. I work for the opposite camp. Then I realized I also had to watch him because he was watching you. It enrages me; I feel as if I am spying on my own shadow under your window, like we're stuck in a painting, the three of us. The Rum and I are the same man with two faces. It makes me crazy to see that he wants to be the paint brush you hold, the dress you wear. I knew what he was up to, but never reported him. How can I report a man who watches you the way I do, my shadow brother? We both want to howl under your window like hungry dogs, yet go about our meaningless lives that everyone else thinks has meaning. I know the bastard. I am he!"

Elena sat like a wall stripped of its paper, pieces of her countenance hanging helplessly in the air, ripped away from their function. She knew everything was exactly as it was before; the sea, the coachman, the cobblestone street. She could hear for the first time, in the moments following Nazım's impassioned declaration, the smallest sounds. They were eerie sounds, which she had never truly noticed before. The clip-clopping of the horses was gone, bits of conversations and the swishing of trees too. She sat still, waiting for those familiar sounds to return, as she heard the hiss of her blood encircling her knuckle joints before rushing to the tips of her fingers. She wondered if this was what the dying heard before the end, all the hidden noises beneath the more boisterous universe everyone took for granted. Then she heard the man beside her exhale and saw him lift his face out of his hands. It all took a few seconds, moving from one universe to the other, and she thought it may have all been imagined.

"I'm so sorry," he muttered. "I don't know what came over me, I did not mean to burden you with all this."

"I'm feeling dizzy," she murmured.

She leaned her head back and closed her eyes, and was immobile. Nazım looked around vaguely at the passing scenery; people crossing streets, vendors pushing carts. It was the same world as this morning, as half an hour ago, the fluid world of anonymous people going about their lives in which he moved about fulfilling his own. Yet now it seemed to him a strange gutted place far removed from anything he knew, which sat inert in the carriage, eyes closed, saying nothing.

Elena tried to focus her mind on familiar things to still the nauseating movement of her mind. An image of Jacob came to her; Jacob smiling with eyes downcast and upper lips hidden under his moustache, elbows leaning on his knees, hands crossed in the air, looking as though he had just heard something that pleased him or was about to share something thrilling with her. It was the first time since his disappearance that Elena saw him unmutilated. She could feel an interior smile spread across her being and everything was still. She held on to this vision a little longer, hoping to return to some place in her existence where it felt joyous and safe to live. The image of her brother started receding and fading upon this thought and out of his upturned, serene lips, a thin stream of blood appeared, snaking down his chin. His eyes were now looking straight at her, blood filling their cups and overflowing down to his cheeks. She saw herself in the dusty train wagon and he was, across from her, dying pitilessly all over again. Her shoulders were held and shaken. She screamed with terror at the sight of a soldier shaking her who then unexpectedly started caressing her head and held her in his arms whispering her name. Her name came in faint echoes that grew closer and closer until she opened her eyes unable to bear the tenderness of her brother's murderer. The eyes of this man who kept repeating her name were familiar and green. The fog in her mind started lifting until she realized she was in the coach, in Nazım's arms, and he was repeating her name with a worried look.

"What . . . ?" her voice barely reached her ears from across a valley.

"You were shaking and screaming, looking into my eyes."

"I had this frightening vision . . . "

She looked around, fearful that the soldier may still be lurking in a corner of the carriage.

"There is no one but me here," he assured her. "Shall I take you to a doctor?"

She straightened herself. "I must have dreamt. I haven't slept much lately, trying to finish the painting. I must have fallen asleep. I'll go home and rest. I'll be fine." She ran her hand over her hair, trying to straighten it out, moved around in her seat. She was still in his arms, their bodies touching all along one leg and shoulder, and their faces were close enough for their breaths to sweep each other's cheeks, although he was now releasing her from his embrace, slowly, the panic-stricken frown on his face not entirely gone. She rested her head on his shoulder. He rubbed her arm gently as if it were a lifeless creature he meant to resuscitate. She placed one cheek near his heart. The sound of its beating brought back old memories. Listening to a man's heartbeat was far more intimate than a kiss, she told him. It was so intimate, it made you think of the most innocent moments in life that cannot even be remembered in images or words, but merely with feelings like this one. When you heard the heartbeat, you knew you belonged to that person. You could perhaps tell a man whose heart you listened to this way that you would love him to your dying moment.

Was kissing entirely out of the question, he wanted to know, since in his case putting his face to her chest might be misinterpreted as lewdness and he did not want to ruin his chances, slight as they might already be. She laughed. For the first time, he saw her small shapely teeth, pink gums, the tip of her tongue, the arch of her throat, happiness cascading out of her in waves. Ah, he sighed with a smile. This, he emphasized, is what I am meant to do in life. To make you laugh. I want nothing else.

"Not even a republic?"

"You can be my sultan, any day. So what is it you'll allow me then, listening to your heart or kissing you?"

She offered parched lips, sensing that what she knew, she might no longer know, after this. He kissed her holding her waist, the way you'd hold a vase filled with flowers.

A Name that Hurts

IN HER ROOM, LATER, she kicked off her shoes and rubbed her sore feet. She opened up her box and took out the reproduction of *Dulle Griet*. She left it on her bedcovers and lay down beside it, looking at the ceiling. She stared at the crack above her bed, shaped like a rabbit almost, one without hind legs or a tail. It had always been there. She wondered how long this house would stand, with the rabbit on her ceiling. Would it outlive her? Would she live here all her life? She wanted to show the man in the crumpled suit her rabbit crack. It was an important detail he would certainly miss by watching her from his window. There were other things too he was bound to miss.

She had listened to the sounds of his heart and also heard the gurgling of his empty stomach in the carriage, which made her smile now. She knew the feel of his lips as well; they had a velvety texture. His long bony fingers had cupped her head as if it were something precious to drink from, to gaze at and admire. There was an invisible conduit from his fingertips to her chest cavity that gave her tiny jolts, electrocutions, making her blood rush, her heart tighten and her soul, which she imagined must have led a cramped existence in that neighbourhood, flutter to her lips in search of an escape. She mused that time would now be measured by the impatient intervals between such jolts. She picked up the reproduction of *Dulle Griet* and held it up, looking at it from her lying position.

She would go to Clementini's tomorrow morning to see if her book on Brueghel had arrived.

When she entered Clementini's store in the bright morning light, the first thing she noticed was that his pigeon hair was gone. He was completely bald, and instead of running back and forth in the aisles of his narrow store he sat on a stool looking melancholy and shrunken. He was looking at the book she had ordered, which had large and gleaming leaves, licking his index finger and turning the pages, occasionally shaking his head from side to side.

"What is it?" she asked him, looking around the empty store.

"When they delivered your Brueghel they took all my books away." He shook his head disconsolately and turned another page, which had the *Dulle Griet* reproduction. "Funny," he said, "how the face of Dulle Griet is in two paintings."

"Which ones?"

"The portrait of the old woman. Did you never notice the resemblance? I think perhaps she was his mother. Or maybe it was his own face? Does she not look like she is running away from this madness? The book says she is mad . . . I don't know," he sighed. "I don't know what to do without my books. How can you keep a store with just one book? I suppose you'll want it too now and then I'll have to shut down my store. Where will I go? What will I do?" He started crying, his face distorted with anxiety, hands cupping his bald head. The book fell down from his lap. Elena picked it up, holding it to her chest.

"You can keep the book if you like," she said.

From the corner of her eye she saw Manolis and Nazım looking through the window side by side. She motioned for them to come in. They looked somewhat identical. She asked them to help Mr Clementini find his books. Manolis took the book and started looking though it.

"Here, the naval battle, why don't you make this sort of thing for my clinic?" he asked, pointing his finger and looking at Elena encouragingly.

"I have other worries now. Give the book back to the man, don't you see he's crying?" she scolded.

Nazım patted Mr Clementini's back, "Mustafa Kemal will find your books," he assured him.

Manolis snapped, "What has Mustafa Kemal got to do with books? What a raving lunatic this communist is!"

Elena put herself between the two men who had raised their fists, shouting at them to stop acting childish.

Mr Clementini looked up, asked Elena if she wanted to pay for it now or in instalments. She shook her head, thinking none of this made any sense, and opened her eyes. She had fallen asleep with her clothes on, still looking up from her bed. The room was drowned in blackness, with grayish humps of various sizes sitting where furniture lived during the day. The corset around her waist was tight; she felt short of breath. Yanking the dress off, she struggled with the hooks in the back, her fingers tripping over each other until she was finished and breathed long and deep before crawling under her covers, placing her hands under her pillow and letting her head sink softly into it. Then she was gone.

In the morning, when the sun came looking for her face through the dark blue linen curtains, she opened her eyes thinking of the man in the crumpled suit, then Manolis and the painting she was commissioned to make. Manolis, enamoured to the point of standing under her window every night to catch a glimpse of her. She felt guilty for not having understood; and annoyed that she knew, now, and could not pretend otherwise.

She rose indolently, not wanting to go anywhere or do anything. Her room was small compared to the others in the house. She had chosen it to be fair, since she was the exclusive user of the attic. Not that anyone had meant to use it before. It had been a dusty depository of objects for which no one saw any utility until she moved in. She allowed no one to go there, to clean or move things without her consent. Her mother, who never bothered with the dustiness of the attic before, made daily comments now about the level of

hygiene in there that left a lot to be desired. It was a woman's corner, and thus had to be neat, was the general gist of her complaint.
She looked under her bed for her slippers and found *Dulle Griet*
instead. She gazed at the mutant creatures, a fish swallowing the
man whose legs were sticking out, the man whose rear end was
actually his mouth, with a spoon sticking out, a group of women
attacking another group; were they mutants, soldiers, it was hard
to tell. A cave in the shape of a man's face with a nose ring, whose
mouth was lined with sharp teeth, was the entrance. Things that
looked like huge eyeballs were nestled in broken eggshell struc-
tures. Strange lizards crawled about. The painting had a brown-
red tinge suggestive of a fire blazing somewhere, with the architecture depicted in the background looking strangely anachronistic,
like some cubist experiment. Griet, the woman in the center of the
painting, did actually look like the subject of another painting, as
Clementini had pointed out in her dream; the portrait of an old
woman. She wondered who it might have been in Brueghel's life.
His wife? His mother? His housekeeper? Himself? She wore a soldier's metal breast plate, albeit loosely, held a spear, a bag, and a
basket of sorts which held a frying pan and kitchen ustensils, and
was hurrying away from a scene where women were butchering
soldiers or creatures that looked like males. She had a bit of a smile
on her face, a vague kind of grin. Actually, a dull, senseless kind of
smirk . . . the kind of involuntary smugness you expected to see in
a mob of faces watching an execution or taking part in a lynching.
In the background, women were killing and pillaging. Was Griet
running off with her spoils towards the mouth of hell? It seemed
that women were the monsters and the men the victims. Was this
his idea of madness? The painting somehow evoked the world she
knew; death and violence everywhere, and humanity at its most
grotesque.

On her way to Clementini's, it occurred to her that perhaps at
the centre of everyone's being was a name that hurt when mentioned. A loss. Something raw around which one endeavoured to

leave a void, by erasing everything related to it. Could this ache, despite all efforts to conceal it from ourselves and make it unmentionable, be the secret architect of our lives, she wondered. Aside from perhaps some children to whom nothing of great significance had happened yet, was there anyone in the world who didn't have such a name? To her it was Jacob's. She looked around at the other pedestrians, the child vendors, the quadruplegic beggars, stocky matrons, reedy soldiers, these waves of nameless people that came and went. Inside them, a core of red, burning grief hiding from the world.

She hurried towards the comfort of Clementini's shop, the smell of the stacks of books, Clementini's ageless energy, as he ran back and forth in search of the right print for the right mind. As she opened the chiming door, she found Clementini crouched, rearranging books on the bottom shelf of a bookcase, his pigeon hair intact, to her relief.

"Ah! La bella Elena!" he exclaimed trying to rise and unbuckle his arthritic knees at the same time.

"Clementini, I'm glad to see nothing has changed in your store." She smiled, content.

"I have to admit," he lifted his finger in the air and waved it as he walked towards his stool, "there are fewer ladies coming in, since the Occupation . . . I hope they are finally sitting at home, reading *Anna Karenina, Madame Bovary* and even *The Idiot*. Yes . . . bought all three; but I never noticed a change in them."

"Did my Brueghel come in?"

"Oh yes, your Brueghel. Very nice reproductions, shiny paper. You'll love it."

He rushed to the back of the store still talking, "I read it already. Good commentary too."

He returned a few seconds later, wiping the dust off a large brown leather bind. "Here. A bit expensive, though. But you can always pay in instalments if you don't have money, or just pay me later."

"You are so good to me Clementini. I'll pay for it, I have the money. I'm actually painting Brueghel copies for Van der Meer and making money."

"The old fart?" Clementini raised his eyebrows.

"No, his son. He's bought a few of my paintings too."

"Ah, the Bolshevik." He smiled enigmatically.

"What do you mean?"

"Nothing . . . I've had a few discussions with him over the years. He's got very interesting views, unlike his father. Very interesting friends too. Also unlike his father."

"Who?"

"Hmm . . . There is this journalist who writes for an obscure paper. He comes here too, occasionally. I've read some of his articles. Passionate sort of chap, wanting to change the world between breakfast and lunch. That type. A lot of thoughts boiling in his head; but the body looks a bit underfed to me. I think he needs to eat more if he wants to change the world and not drop dead. But anyway, Van der Meer and this fellow are inseparable."

"Hmm . . . hmmm . . . " She shook her head listening to him while flipping through the pages of her new book.

"Do they come here together?"

"They go everywhere together; exhibitions, concerts, speeches . . . "

"Aha, I see . . . " she mumbled, still apparently engrossed in her new book.

"You do?"

"Uh?"

"Keep reading your book, I'll go back to my shelf."

He crouched down with difficulty. "Pass me that cushion on the stool there."

She put it on the floor in front of him so he could rest his knees.

"At my age you need a cushion for everything; one for behind, one for the neck, one for the knees . . . Don't be surprised if you start seeing more cushions than books around here in time. I should retire, sell the shop. There is this young fellow who's eyeing it. He wants to sell zippers and buttons and ladies' undies and that sort of stuff. Now with yet another war going on, I don't know who will read books . . . "

"Schools will always need books. I will always need your books," she said, her voice coming out a little panicked.

"Nobody has money to buy books. Except you, it seems. Finding a fresh egg and being able to pay for it is the great feat these days. Books will soon be thrown in the fireplace for heating. Those who bought *War and Peace* will be grateful; it will keep them warm for at least half an hour. So will *Brothers Karamazov.*"

"What would you do with your time?" said Elena. "Sit at home and think about your aches and pains. I wouldn't sell the shop if I were you. You've survived a war already, you'll survive this one too."

He said nothing, continued rearranging the books on the bottom shelf. She took out money from her purse and put it in his drawer.

"I've put it in there," she pointed. "I have to go now." With the book under her arm, she headed for the door. On the way she turned around and asked, "So, when were you thinking of closing shop?"

"One of these days . . . But we'll see each other before that. I won't close without taking leave from you, bella."

She gave a little wave as she opened the door, and with the small bells chiming, she was gone.

Elena walked back home feeling depressed about the world. She climbed up the front stairs of the house and opened the door, letting it slam back inadvertently, wincing at the noise. A few moments later her mother shouted from somewhere inside the house: "Elena?"

"Yes, I'm sorry!" she shouted back.

"Come here, I need to talk to you."

Elena went towards the kitchen, where her mother was stirring a boiling pot containing white shirts and underclothes to be washed. The air was steamy and fragrant with olive soap. "Niko is sick," Marie said, looking up from the foaming, bubbling liquid. "He's got a fever and a rash. Doesn't look good. Pol is keeping him company in bed now. Can you go get Manolis?"

Scarlatine

ELENA RUSHED BACK OUT the door in search of Manolis.

Upstairs, Niko lay in bed, glassy-eyed, with rashes all over his face and hands, and listening to his uncle, whose notion of human interaction was inspired by geometry. People, he explained to Niko, were like points, relating to one another on a plane, from hexagons, triangles, squares, and the like. There were those that were on parallel figures that skewed to infinity, others who had an infinite number of points between them, though apparently very close. You may have been part of a hexagon without knowing who the others were in the bigger picture. In Polycarp's mental universe nothing was left to chance and everything worked according to rules and equations he was yet to define. His picture resembled a map of stars on a dark night, the contemplation of which invariably left the young boy overwhelmed. Could the horrors he witnessed have been explained by those rules?

"I am just a quasi-thinker, my boy," he responded, smiling sadly, "trying to find my way out of a maze, but I'm most likely trapped in one of my own making . . . "

"Why did this happen, then?" Niko demanded. "That little girl I saw, wearing her Sunday dress, why did she have to be killed the day the Greek army came?"

He shrugged.

"Countless little girls in Sunday dresses have been senselessly killed, long before we were born. And there will be many more, long after we have died. If there is an answer to this, I have not found it, Niko . . . I've only read a few books, that's all." He added, almost to himself, "this is probably something you should ask one of your friars. They're the experts of the whys and wherefores. They'll tell you why God wanted it so, or didn't interfere with it, or whatever it is they say nowadays . . . "

"But how can you live without an answer?"

"With much doubt and trepidation."

He walked out of the room and returned with a book. "This is Ömer Hayyam." He shook the book in the air before opening it to a page he already seemed to have memorized. "He says the world, the universe, the stars . . . it is all emptiness." His long fingers fluttered about before landing on the rust-coloured book cover. "In this universe that endlessly constructs and deconstructs, it is but one breath you will take, and that is also emptiness . . . Read it." Long pale fingers offered the book.

"I'm nauseous, I can't read," sighed Niko, feeling the walls in his room closing in on him. The grooves on the door of the big brown armoire were swelling and wagging like fleshy fingers. He closed his eyes. In his ears, the words "endlessly constructs and deconstructs" kept repeating in a loop. "Uncle, I'm not well."

His uncle caressed his arm and told him Manolis would soon come and help him feel better.

"But . . . you always say . . . he is useless," objected Niko.

"Sure he is; he can't play tavla if his life depended on it, he wouldn't know if a painting was hanging upside down. But he's a good doctor, I'm sure. He has to be good at something, eh?" he smiled.

Marie had come up the stairs with the small pewter bowl they used when they took baths. It was filled with water and vinegar, and a grey washcloth floated on it. She sat by the side of his bed and gave him cool compresses, whispering tenderly in Greek, "Hrisomou, moromou . . . " Please get well, she implored. She called on her son Jacob to help his little boy. She sang him the lullaby his father would sing to him. Niko fell asleep.

Elena arrived at Manolis's front door. The shutters were all closed. She knocked a few times and waited for Manolis to appear. She wondered what to do next. She did not know at which hospital to go looking for him. She thought of Nazım. Surely he would know somebody. She hurried towards his house and knocked on his door. He opened the door, shirt sticking out of his floating pants, his hair slightly dishevelled. When he saw Elena at the door, he quickly stuffed his shirt in his pants and tried to straighten his hair, apologizing for his looks.

"I was taking a nap," he smiled.

"My nephew is sick. I need a doctor. My friend is not there; I don't know where to go."

He hesitated, taking in the flushed cheeks, the bosom heaving up and down breathlessly, the half-parted lips he desired, the eyes that met his and escaped. He stood there, gazing.

"Do you?" he heard and realized he was required to answer. He nodded and disappeared inside before coming out with his jacket and hat, which he quickly adjusted, and down the road they went, half running. He looked clownish, with his uncombed hair, the white shirt sticking out from under his jacket in places, the hat sitting gingerly on his mass of wild hair. "We'll go to my doctor," he explained. "He is on Rue des Roses. He's got a car. . . we can ride back with him."

By the time they reached the gate of the doctor's house they were completely out of breath. The garden was fragrant with roses and jasmine. The name Dr M Bankman was engraved on a shingle beside the doorbell.

The doctor was a very tall man. His head reached the top of the door frame, and the white napkin hanging down from his collar looked ridiculously small for his size. He was in the midst of having his supper. Children's noises came from inside. He excused himself and hurried inside to get his jacket and bag, wiping his mouth and discarding the napkin as he hurried away. A few minutes later he was back at the door, ready to go see Niko.

They drove on the empty streets to Elena's home. Niko opened his eyes and gave a frightened look, seeing a stanger in front of him suddenly.

"Hello, young man, what have we got here?" asked the doctor standing by Niko's bedside. The doctor checked his tonsils, looked into his eyes and ears, felt his neck with his hand, and placed the cold stethoscope on his back and listened. He was not wasting any time. His movements were fluid, as if choreographed. He then stuck a thermometer in the boy's mouth and checked his pulse.

"Scarlatine," he declared. "One month of bed rest. Here's a syrup. No school, young man, I bet it breaks your heart . . . "

He scrawled something on a piece of paper and gave further instructions.

Elena thanked the doctor and opened her purse as they moved towards the door. Nazım held her hand and pressed it down to indicate he would take care of it. "I'll find out which pharmacy is open tonight. I'll get the syrup, just give me the prescription. You stay here, with the boy," he said to her in a hushed tone. Elena nodded, smiling faintly. He was taking charge like a protector, she thought. He squeezed her hand in a quick and hidden move, reminding her of their complicity, and was gone, following the storky gait of the doctor down the stairs and into the street.

Polycarp was behind her as she closed the door. He looked at her, nodding with a smile. She defended herself with a question, "What are you smiling about?"

He shrugged and headed towards the living room. She followed.

"I think you may want to hear a story." He lifted his head to listen to the sounds upstairs, making sure his mother was busy with Niko.

"What story?"

"About your new friend."

She frowned. "He's not my new friend!"

"A pity." He picked up the book lying on the coffee table and opened it, as he prepared to sit down.

"Go ahead and tell your story, then," she said and threw herself on the sofa. "Is it a true story or are you going to make it up?"

He laughed. "Who knows with me? I can't always tell the difference . . . Do you want to hear it anyway?"

She nodded, feigning nonchalance as she stretched her legs in front of her.

"Nazım," he began in a hushed voice, "was born in Izmir, the only son of a well-respected general in the Sultan's army. His parents had an arranged marriage, as custom demanded. Jülide Hanım, that was his mother's name, I think, was the daughter of a military man as well, and although illiterate, she knew how to run a household, which was all that was expected of her."

"Where do you get all these details?" she interrupted.

"Do you want to listen or not?"

She nodded.

"The first child, Nazım, was born, and all was well. They hired a wetnurse, and later on a governess. The governess was a pretty young girl of Greek origin, by the name of Miriam, whose parents did not have the means to support her. They had many mouths to feed, and Miriam, who was fifteen at the time, was placed in the general's home, to earn her living. The general and his wife treated her kindly. She supped at their table and taught their son the Greek language.

"All was well until she became pregnant. The mystery father was never revealed. There were tears and shame as her belly grew with new life. Her family rejected her. The general and his wife, however, took her under their wing and told her they would welcome her child into their family. A girl was born to Miriam, and was given the name Despina. She and Nazım grew up in the same household, raised like brother and sister for a few years. As time went by, Despina's resemblance to the general became flagrant, and consequently Jülide Hanım's behaviour towards Miriam and her child took on a rancor which made it impossible for them to coexist under the same roof. Gossip about the general's indiscretion began to spread. He took to drinking and started avoiding his home altogether. Miriam and her daughter found themselves on the street one morning with nowhere to go. No other household would hire a governess with the general's illegitimate child in tow, and certainly no one would marry her in this dishonoured state. Somehow they set up house in a dingy neighbourhood, and it was said the general secretly paid for Miriam's expenses.

"She continued having the general's frequent visits, but in time, he brought his drinking partners along. They brought her lavish presents. She moved to a larger home in Kokaryalı. The general eventually died of cirrhosis. Miriam, having lost her financial support, turned to the general's friends. They obliged, in return for her favours. Her house became known to many and in a few years business became too brisk for Miriam to handle on her own. She took in a few more girls and created a lucrative commerce, providing amusement for the rich and famous men of Smyrna. Hers was the only place of its kind in town, with a baby grand piano in its waiting room. It was even said that many deals, political and otherwise, were first reached in the House with the Piano before making their way to respectable halls. Despina began to work there too once she reached the age of sixteen. She was the prized one, due to her beauty; the one reserved for the best clients."

"Is this all true?" Elena asked in disbelief.

"I think so. Do you want me to stop?"

"No! But why are you telling me all this?"

"I thought you might want to know."

"Keep going. But let me make one thing very clear first ... "

"I know, I know." he cut in. "He is not your friend. So I continue?"

She nodded feeling queasy.

"Meanwhile, Nazım was packed off to a boarding school in Switzerland. He befriended the young Van der Meer, who had also been packed off there by his parents. It turns out that Nazım was a bit too hot-headed for his Swiss school's liking and eventually got the boot. That story you already know. He and Van der Meer became involved in a communist group. Van der Meer despised his father's bourgeois life. He was also very attached to Nazım, whose own ideas were fuelled by the condescension he encountered in Europe as an Ottoman. His ideas took on a nationalistic tinge, what with the Young Turks already on the scene working against the Sultan, and the War breaking out. He wanted to make a difference when he returned from Switzerland. As soon as he got home, he used his connections in Russia to finance a communist newspaper. Nobody knew he was the brains behind it, and someone else ran the paper. He also joined a revolutionary underground movement to which Mustafa Kemal belonged.

"Mustafa Kemal was already a persona non grata in Istanbul. The Sultan and the Young Turks wanted to do away with him, even though he was the most brilliant military commander in the Ottoman army, the hero of Gallipoli. They tried, and so far seem to have failed. Kemal has a following and secretly moved inland to put together the army now fighting the Entente and the Greeks who have invaded Izmir. You know all this, of course, and I digress . . . Van der Meer returned to Izmir and joined Nazım's movement heart and soul."

"What about Despina? Is she still around? Does he know she's his sister?"

Polycarp nodded. "When he returned, he found out why he was sent to Europe in such a hurry. Everybody in his parents' circle knew about it. He wasn't told what had happened to his half-sister, but found out soon enough. He was heartbroken. Got it into his head that he would get her out of her predicament.

"Despina, meanwhile, having acquired a cynical, bilious disposition, regarded him as a soulful idiot, and a nuisance to boot. She refused to see him when he went knocking on her door. So he took to paying his way. He'd pay to see her, bring her books to read, promised to take care of her if she left her sordid life. I suppose she felt he should pay for their father's sins. With time, she came around a little. She listens to him now, having realized he is not so easy to dismiss. He continues to educate her, in his own way, and she belongs to his secret organization, as a spy . . . "

"How do you know all this? If this is common knowledge, then their days are numbered. I'm surprised you speak so freely of this."

"I'm his friend, remember? And I trust you will not breathe a word of this to anyone. I thought it was important for you to know, since you seem to have embarked on something."

"Whatever gave you that idea?"

"The secret hand-squeezing at the door. Be very careful."

The book he had picked up before telling his story was still in his hands, his index finger stuck in. He opened it, making himself comfortable in the armchair. Elena observed him quietly. It irritated her, the way he always seemed to be a step ahead. At the same time she felt safe knowing he was paying attention on her behalf.

"I will," she said simply.

Niko had many feverish nights, not at all alleviated by compresses and lullabies. Marie, Polycarp, and Elena took turns sitting by his bedside as he moaned and tossed. When he opened his eyes he was reassured to find someone close by watching over him. The images inside his head were tamer, behaving according to laws he recognized. But once, when his grandmother had given him a sip of water and as he lay back on the bed, having thanked her, he went on to explain that his mother and father were waiting for him by the door and he had to go. It was a beautiful sunny day outside, the way you know it from the birds' joyous twittering. His parents were in their Sunday attire, his mother wearing a bright turquoise chiffon hat. They were motioning him to follow. He grabbed his cap and ran down the stairs after them, thinking her hat would be easy to spot in a crowd, and he would not get lost.

"Mama, you look lovely!" he said as he tried to reach them. She turned, her eyes somewhat hidden under the hat, and smiled at him, the way only a mother could, and he felt a burst of joy inside his chest, realizing he had a mother whose smile he recognized, regardless of what everyone else thought. They walked along the Quay, licking ice cream cones. His mother's was turquoise and matched her hat, making him wonder what kind of fruit flavour that was. As if reading his thoughts, she said, without turning to him, "It is made of sea foam, you should try it." He looked at his own cone and instead of ice cream, there was a gleaming yellow lemon stuck in it. It was bitter to lick. He was in a crowded amusement park, an immense ferris wheel going round and round beside him. When he looked down, he had lost his parents. He searched in the dense crowd for his mother's turquoise hat but could not see it. He started running and calling her name in vain. He had lost her in a moment's distraction. He looked up at the ferris wheel again and noticed his parents at the very top, talking with each other and laughing, ignoring him completely, as though he did not exist. He sat on the ground weeping.

"Niko, Niko!" He lifted his head to find his grandmother's worried face bent over him. "It's all right, my boy, you're not alone, I'm here." She caressed his head. "And you'll be fine, I promise you." She wiped his wet cheeks.

"I think I'm going to die, Grandma," he said with difficulty.

"Hush, don't be silly. I had it too, at your age, and look at me, I'm still standing."

She proceeded to count his orifices and crossed herself. Counting the orifices, of which there were nine according to her, was something that had to be done to children as soon as there was any danger of a jinx. It had something to do with the devil not being able to enter from the holes if you counted them all quickly enough. He wasn't sure how it worked, but this was his first lesson in anatomy. A human has nine holes in total. Later, when he discovered that girls had an extra one, he challenged his grandmother. She was adamant the tenth one did not count. She crossed herself. He explained to her he suspected his mother might have died because nobody had counted that extra orifice, the one that brought him into the world. She crossed herself again and told him to stop speaking of shameful things.

"Is it shameful to have babies?" he asked.

"Certainly. Very improper!"

"If so, why did you have three?"

It was his first victory using logic against superstition. Still, he expected to have his nine orifices counted at the first sign of danger.

A candle was flickering on his dresser in front of an icon of the Virgin Mary. Her long oval face looked melancholic and dolorous. In the palm of her hand, Jesus did not look like a child, but a miniature man, one thin hand wrapped around his mother's neck. He had a pained look in his eyes as well, knowing that sometime soon she would let him walk to his death, as foretold. There was no room for maneuvering for this particular child, whose father was the Omnipotent, but at least, for the time being, he could sit in the comfort of her motherly palm like other children his age.

The icon was hundreds of years old and was only brought out in extremely grave situations. Thus, he concluded, his was a case that required the Virgin's intervention. Having let her own son die (there was no arguing with God), Niko presumed she was expected to try harder to save other people's children. Her own sweet lamb resided in heaven doing God's work. He was tender and forgiving and kind, having inherited his mother's best qualities. It was all rather confusing, having the Father and the Son in heaven and also the Holy Ghost, all three being one and the same. No wonder everyone lit candles to the Virgin Mary and prayed to her. She was the mother of all, and stood apart, uninvolved in the hierarchy of fathers and sons, doing all the hard work, the way mothers generally did. She was the real thing, like his grandma, and together they guarded his orifices from evil.

He drifted once again into a deep slumber, hushed voices coming to his ears from faraway places to remind him that he had not yet died.

Dr Bankman was back, wanting to stick his cold stethoscope on Niko's chest, when he opened his eyes. His grandmother entered the room holding a boiled syringe in its steaming metal box, between thick towels. This visit did not augur well.

"I don't need a needle," he protested, "I'm feeling much better."

The doctor ignored him. "I want you to get up and go to the bathroom. You will pee in this glass jar and bring it back to me."

He handed Niko the jar and helped him get up. Elena supported him by the armpits and walked him to the bathroom. He felt his kneecaps knock each other with each step he took. And he did get the needle as soon as he offered the jar with dark yellow pee to the doctor. With a heavy heart he watched the doctor squirt some of the medicine from the syringe into the air, then slowly bring down his arm, rub his buttock with a damp piece of cotton and prick it. It was painful but he bit his lip the way a man should, as the doctor recommended, and it was over. As he gathered his instruments, Dr Bankman declared he'd give him a daily injection for the rest of the week. Niko wanted to cry like a braying donkey when he heard this, but his recently earned manhood precluded such shows of weakness. He nodded and turned his back to everyone.

Nazım was waiting downstairs, by now a regular at the house in the evenings, exchanging pleasantries with Polycarp as Dr Bankman came down the stairs, knees going in and out like enormous scissors, followed by Elena, who was wringing her hands in anxiety. Everyone wanted to know the oracle of the urine jar. Dr Bankman indicated the results would be ready the next day around noon. If the kidneys were not involved, the illness would simply run its course and he'd improve. However, if they were involved, the boy's life would be in grave danger, and he would require hospitalization. Nazım followed the doctor out, volunteering to get the results from the doctor's office the next morning.

As they closed the door, Polycarp turned to Elena. "Funny thing...Manolis has not been to see Niko at all." In Aya Katerina, where everyone knew everyone else, this was bizarre indeed.

"I'll go look if he's home," said Polycarp, putting on his vest. The night air was starting to get cool and dewy, announcing the stealthy arrival of autumn.

The Stranger

MANOLIS WAS NOT AT HOME. The closed doors and shutters indicated that there had been a planned departure, and Polycarp wondered why their friend had not advised them of his trip. The dog was obviously gone too, indicating that the absence would not be a short one. As he walked away in the clear starry night, he thought he should visit Manolis's clinic the next day, for signs of where he might have gone.

He decided to take a long walk, aimlessly, through the narrow streets of this neighbourhood where he was born and where he suspected he would also die. He had never left it. Smyrna was his universe: the Quay, Rue de France, Fasula, the various quarters, Cordelio, Bayrakli. And yet he felt as though his life had somehow abandoned him here and gone elsewhere. Absurd thought. Where else could he have lived, how else could his life have turned out? In this tiny corner of the universe, civilization followed civilization, leaving a column here, tossing a coin there, reminders that would last longer than cheekbones or hands, or a look that made your heart tremble. Infinity would elude you in a small quarter of Smyrna no less than it would on the majestic heights of a mountain elsewhere. He gazed at the lights in the windows—people living with their accumulations of habits and objects they called lives. Time would sweep everything away, a formidable wind, to create another, unrecognizeable landscape within the span of a century or even less. No one would remember any of this—the way streets smelled, the look of these gleaming cobblestones on which his feet made tiny echoes, the families living in these houses, each with a hundred stories to tell. It occurred to him that perhaps we started looking for our lives from the time we were born, the way you look for your glasses, knowing they are here somewhere, yet unable to locate them.

He turned a corner and realized he was walking towards the Quay. All roads in Smyrna led to the sea; even those parallel to it were crossed by innumerable side streets and alleys, inviting you to change course at every corner, blowing a whiff of iodine your way and the tiny glopping sounds of the water. At the Quay someone would always be fishing with a line, seated on a small straw stool. And now, in the late hours of the evening, a man who looked like he had been sitting there all day, was holding the line and squinting ahead. What could he want to see at this hour of the night, Polycarp marvelled as he passed by. Did he not realize the sun had gone? Were these fishermen you encountered at all times of the day fishing for their lost lives in the depths of the sea? A blue-eyed Laz fisherman from the Black Sea once explained to him that all fishermen were philosophers. They quietly conversed with the sea and skies about life.

The life of a fisherman is a silent one. If you talk, the fish get scared. So you think instead. You daydream. You tell stories in your head. It's a good life, thought Polycarp, but you cannot read books. They get wet, you get distracted. Not for me. He enjoyed telling stories, when he found the thread. It frequently happened that he couldn't find the thread of a single sentence. There were times he needed to read something over and over because he could not focus his mind.

He looked up from his reverie. Some hundred metres away stood a man whose back, turned towards him, made him think of Jacob. He was wearing a dark blue jacket with sagging pockets, exactly like Jacob's when he used to work in the hat shop. His hair was blond too. He was walking slowly. Polycarp's heart jolted. He decided to follow the man, hoping he would turn his head towards him, so he could see the face. The man kept walking, and Polycarp followed. He quickened his steps. Strangely, the man walked faster too, widening the distance. They speed-walked this way, meandering through the quiet dim streets. Polycarp felt nervous but was unable to quit. The man stopped suddenly, having reached his destination. He stood in front of the steps of the Church of St Polycarp, and seemed to wait for Polycarp to approach. The light from the street lamp shone on the soft waves of his blond hair. The jacket was Jacob's, Polycarp was sure of this now, in the light. This jacket, until this morning, had hung from a hook at the shop, the way Jacob had left it. He wondered now if the man had stolen it.

"Hey you!" Polycarp called out.

The man did not turn. He simply vanished. Polycarp ran in all directions to find him, finally realizing that he was completely alone. He walked inside the church and was greeted by the smell of melting wax and incense. Large marble slabs lay on the floor, with dates and names. Some as old as the pestilence. He sat in the last row to catch his breath and looked around the hall in the candle-light. The last time he had been here was during childhood, on Good Friday. People standing in a queue to kiss the feet of Christ on the cross; monotonous Latin chants and the sadness permeating the place, the paintings all concealed by purple drapes. The colour of mourning, the smell of incense, and the chiming of the little bell to tell you when to kneel. Rituals to keep the pious busy.

The centrepiece in the church depicted the martyrdom of St Polycarp. It was during the reign of Marcus Aurelius, on February 23, 115, that the eighty-six-year-old bishop of Smyrna was hunted down and captured on the second floor of a small house, having been betrayed by a servant. He went down the stairs, slowly, deliberately, to greet the Romans who had come to arrest him. A beloved man of steadfast faith, albeit in the wrong religion.

He was taken to the stadium perhaps right here where the church now stood. A fragile old man, barefoot, wearing a white robe, looking like a Greek philosopher. The blue veins under his parchment skin crawled up and down his body gasping for air, bent like a centennial olive, his white feet bleeding.

The soldiers led him gently to the pyre, the way you do a beloved grandfather. From the look on their faces, St Polycarp had said something kind to them and they were mortified at the task they were to perform.

One of them whispered to him, "Just say what they want to hear, old man, no one knows the inside of your heart. They will let you go."

The old man continued walking. He stood on the pyre, his hands bound behind him. He was asked again to swear by the fortune of Caesar and refused.

"Bring forth what you will," he said.

The soldiers lit up the pyre, flames licked at his flesh like burning tongues. The spectators saw him, with his hair and beard intact and his skin a golden hue, then a wind came and blew away the fire. He was gone.

Polycarp gazed at the painting a long time, recalling this event that took place seventeen hundred years ago. It was inside him, this memory of something he had never witnessed. In the foreground was the suffering of a very old and wise man who refused to retract and conform. The glory of suffering was already present in the very seditious act of burning at the stake for one's beliefs. In the background was the rule of Rome, in disarray, as it tried to affirm its might, making daily spectacles of atrocities. A tradition faithfully passed from one civilization to the next, one religion to the other, he mused. Intolerance, the collective sin, ritualized and absolved by whomever needed to prove their might. The demand for an enemy was ever present. He rose and left the vacant church, his steps echoing in the dark corners behind the fluted columns. He shuddered, remembering Jacob's double who had brought him here. Pushed by a sudden fear, he ran out into the moonlit night and kept running until he reached the steps of the house.

Light was coming from Niko's window and above that, from the attic. He climbed up the stairs to find Marie putting compresses on Niko's forehead. She was hunched over, her long white hair flowing down to her waist, the top of her head glowing in the light of the candles. The smell of vinegar filled the room. Upstairs in the attic Elena had started the new painting, having already outlined roughly in pencil, and was applying the background colours of red and ochre. Dulle Griet was already there, as a shadow of herself, soon to acquire movement and her stupid grin.

"Why did you choose this one?" he asked, sitting down on the last step.

She shrugged. "I don't know, really. On impulse, I suppose . . . "

"I was at St Polycarp's just now. Followed a man who was wearing Jacob's work jacket. Thought he was a thief. He disappeared in front of the church. Just vanished into thin air. He looked like Jacob too, same fair hair, though I never saw his face. I tried to pass him to get a look, but he wouldn't let me, he walked very fast and never once turned to look at me. How is Niko doing?"

"Still feverish. She's been putting compresses on him ever since you left. Won't let me take over. She intends to spend the night awake beside him. I figured painting will keep me awake. You think it was some kind of hallucination?"

"It seemed real to me. But then again, it always does. Why of all places to the Church of St Polycarp? I mean, aside from the obvious name connection? If I were hallucinating about my brother, why wouldn't he take me to places where we played as children, instead of this ancient place that gives me the creeps? Besides, I've been feeling fine in my head lately."

"You're worried about the boy. Maybe that's why . . . " She continued filling in the basic shapes, a dark stain here a lighter tone there.

"Do you think he'll pull through? I think I'll go relieve Mother for a bit. She has been looking so frail lately."

He disappeared down the stairs without waiting for a response.

Niko was sleeping, his mouth slightly open, letting out a tiny whistle with every breath. Polycarp managed to convince his mother to go sleep a little, he would call if something changed. She rubbed her back as she walked towards her bedroom. Polycarp sat by Niko's bed and changed the compress on his forehead. The boy's cheeks were still red. Polycarp caressed his soft hair. Niko half opened his eyes.

"Aha!" smiled Polycarp, "There you are!"

The boy tried to smile through his chapped and swollen lips.

Polycarp rubbed the boy's limp hand. "The friars have been asking about you, you know. Especially Frère Felix, he says nobody can play the piccolo like you. The other boys have sausage fingers that don't bend fast enough. They also have sausage meat for brains. He`s threatened to come and visit you. I hastened to tell him it wouldn't be necessary, of course. You'd be up and about in a couple of days. Look, you've got pink cheeks already. A bit of broth and you'll be fit as a fiddle."

"Is there any?" asked Niko, remembering hunger.

"Well!" exclaimed Polycarp, "I'll go wake up the butcher this minute!"

Polycarp ran to awaken Marie, who opened her eyes and screamed, "What happened to him?" Polycarp calmed her, explaining that the boy was hungry.

Marie sprang out of bed, to go see for herself. She saw that Niko's eyes had lost the fog which had clouded them for weeks.

"Are you hungry?" she asked. He nodded. "I'll go make you something right away!" she said and flew down the stairs like a child. Soon they could hear her singing and the clanging of pots in the kitchen.

The next morning when Nazım showed up at the door, clean-shaven and perfumed, Polycarp smiled and said, "I think that test came out clean, am I right?"

Nazım was surprised. "How could you tell?"

"Come in, see for yourself."

Nazım was led up the stairs to Niko's room. He stood in the doorway gingerly and waved at Niko, who smiled back. His temperature was almost normal now, and he was regaining his energy. There were an open encyclopedia on the bedcovers and some story books. Polycarp led Nazım up to Elena's studio and left. Elena put down her brushes. She moved some papers and books from the chair to the floor for Nazım to sit down.

"I won't stay long," he hastened to say.

"It was so good of you to help so much with my nephew's illness. We are forever indebted to your kindness." She wiped her hands on her skirt. "Let me make you some tea . . . if we still have some. I'll go check." She moved to go down the stairs.

He held her wrist, "Sit."

It came out almost as a whisper, causing her to shiver. She sat on a stool a bit farther away.

"I need to tell you something, and then I'll leave. You probably know enough about my family by now. Your brother must have told you."

She breathed in, trying to emit sounds of protest, but he cut in, "As I hope he would, being a good brother. I would completely understand if you wanted to stop seeing me. I have the family I do and I need to live with it all. I don't want you to be part of my messy life. I'm sorry about the carriage. I shouldn't have . . . "

He rose to go.

"Sit down."

He turned around to look at her.

"It's my turn," she was firm. "I'm truly sorry about your sister's predicament. But it is not something you caused. Your father's guilt is not yours to carry. I admire you for trying to help her. I'm honoured to call you my friend. Don't apologize about the carriage. I . . . I hope to share one with you again someday."

"Elena, there's something else . . . I'm leaving soon. I don't know how it will turn out. The war, I mean. Battles are being fought inland and I must go. I can't write anything. They won't let me. I feel useless and . . . crushed living in this occupied city where I'm made to feel like a stranger. You understand . . . But as long as you live in it, I have a reason to come back. And my sister, well, she . . . " He sighed. "I don't want to bore you with all this."

"Please . . . Go on," she urged.

"I've done everything I could; found her a place in Ankara, where she will be away from all this, where she can start a new life. I got Van der Meer to arrange for her to go to Switzerland where I still have some friends. She will not budge from here. 'This is my life' she says, 'I don't know how else to live.' She hopes one of those rich generals will marry her, take her to Greece, Italy, Istanbul, wherever it is they come from, buy her fur coats and silk stockings, houses by the sea. Beneath her cynicism, she seems so naïve to me."

He shook his head sadly. "I am all she's got in this world. If I die, if things get bad for her, and she needs help, Van der Meer has promised to do his best. Anyway . . . you hardly know me."

Her face had turned pale. "When are you leaving, then?"

"A week from now."

"Let's go for a walk," she said, the words shaping themselves blandly and falling out of her mouth. "Give me five minutes to go change."

She went down the stairs holding on to the railing like an elderly person afraid of a false step.

Soon she was back and they walked out into the street.

"Let's find a carriage, then," she smiled faintly, "let's walk farther. I don't want anyone to see us." A few blocks away, Nazım whistled for a coach and helped her get on.

"Where to?" asked the driver.

"Take us in the direction of Kokaryalı, we'll tell you where to go from there."

He picked up her hand as it lay huddled on her lap like a wounded bird. "I'm sorry, Elena."

"Are you?" She nodded. "Where are we going?"

"Kokaryalı, where the House with the Piano is. I'll show it to you from outside, so you know. It's a beautiful area. We can also go farther, much farther and never come back."

"You mean take a boat to an island?" She smiled.

"We wouldn't get very far with all those warships around, I fear. I think we should stick to a coach ride for today."

"My brother was taken away. He never came back."

"I know."

"Of course you do." She looked at him. "He did not have a choice. You do. Why are you in such a rush to get killed?"

"I hope not to get killed."

"Then you will kill. How can you bear it?"

"How can I bear sitting in this city that has been transformed into a shadow of itself. Can you bear it? Who's going to do something about it?"

"Don't you see that it is obscene, that you will murder someone who probably has children back in Greece and did not ask to be here in the first place?"

"He will murder people who never asked their land to be occupied, their wives to be raped, their children to be skewered. Elena are we here to argue?"

"I don't know why we're here. We're here because you will be gone in one week. Because we never got to know each other, and because we may die a few weeks or months from now."

She continued, her cheeks now the colour of fury, "And you claim you're in love with me. Wanting to howl under my window. Isn't that what you said? And I'm . . . and I'm to remain here wondering every hour if this was your last. No one will ever come to tell me you're dead. You should have never . . . How dare you make me wait for you?"

She ripped her hand away from his and turned aside. Tears rolled down her cheeks. She wiped them away with her sleeves.

"Give me your handkerchief!" she ordered, looking away. He

took out his white handkerchief, neatly folded and pressed, with his initials on it. She blew her nose. He took her in his arms.

"Please stay," she whispered, "please stay for me."

"You'll keep that handkerchief and think of me," he said. "At least I hope you will keep it, now that you've used it so liberally." He smiled and kissed her forehead. It made her smile.

"I should give it back to you like this, so you'll remember me.' she replied trying to stick it back into his pocket. He wrestled her away as she giggled. He caressed her face and kissed her nose, whispering her name like a prayer.

They had been unaware of the passing scenery. The horses were pulling them through Kokaryalı, where the villas lining the seaside had beautiful wrought iron doors decorated with vines and gargoyles. Rose bushes and bougainvillea hung heavily over the garden walls. They trotted past the synagogue with its light blue windows. Then the bakery that used to make fresh gevrek, wheelshaped rolls, sprinkled with sesame seeds. They were crisp, with a long aftertaste. The bakery was now vacant. There were two old loaves of bread in the window. Something desolate had crept into the scenery. It was hard to tell that this was the neighbourhood where people sat on their terraces in the summer, having tea parties.

"Here it is," he pointed. She looked over at the villa. It did not look particularly striking to her. The garden was well kept, the gate closed.

"Here she lives. Do you know that there is a song about her? It's partly Turkish, partly Greek, like her. My sister has not had much of a childhood. It horrifies me to think of it. At the age of sixteen, sold to the highest bidder; some rich fat pervert no doubt, while I was completely oblivious. My father was a coward. He was good to me, and a hero whom I admired, with all his medals and shiny swords. I grew up thinking him the best and greatest of men. Meanwhile he was some rich fat pervert himself, taking advantage of a young needy governess in his house. It is easy to say, 'You are not guilty of your father's sins.' Not so easy to believe. When my sister tells me she hates men, it is as though she's slapping me in the face and I feel I deserve it."

They had left the city far behind. On one side were yellow fields guarded by scarecrows, and on the other, waves crashing into mossy rocks.

"How far do you want me to go?" asked the driver, slowing down the horses.

They were nearing Clasomeni, the sunken city where Homer was said to have lived. Rolling hills covered with olive and fig groves were punctuated here and there by a tile roof the colour of peaches. Seagulls with piercing cries drew ellipses around the fishermen's boats. Some stood guard on the highest rocks, waiting for the spray to settle before swooping down for sardines.

"We'll go to a teahouse for a little while. I'll offer you lunch if you wait for us," he told the driver.

The driver smiled a toothless grin. "Hey, I'm not in a rush to go anywhere. Fine with me."

He pulled the horses to the side of the road for them to get off. The teahouse was among the fields, separated from the surrounding meadow by a low wall of rounded grey rocks. There were wooden tables and chairs in the shades provided by oaks and willows. The teahouse itself was painted with white chalk. A few goats were feeding peacefully in the meadow. Elena looked all around, took a deep breath.

Nazım offered, "We can return tomorrow if you wish. Bring your easel. We can spend the day here. Have a picnic." Elena's smile was radiant, like one who has unexpectedly received a present.

They spent the day walking up and down country roads, occasionally resting under a tree. When they returned to the city, Nazım arranged for the driver to pick them up again the next morning. They got off the coach a few blocks away from their neighbourhood and walked separately until they got home. She walked on one sidewalk, he on the opposite one. Once in a while they glanced at each other furtively and smiled, and nodded their goodbyes before entering their respective houses.

"Where were you all these hours?" her mother demanded.

"Out and about. I actually decided to go to Cordelio to get my advance from Van der Meer for the painting," she lied.

"You look like you've been in the sun."

"I had the sun in my face sitting in the tramway" she replied, climbing the stairs two at a time to her attic.

She came down. "Oh, and by the way, I met my old friend Camelia from my school days. She lives in Cordelio too. She invited me to spend the day there. I accepted. It'll be a nice change for me. I may take my easel and paint a little in her garden."

Marie thought it a little strange that her savage daughter had cared to socialize all of a sudden, but felt hopeful that she might meet her future husband by being out and about.

The next day Elena looked at the size of her easel and decided simply to take a pad, and charcoal. She put them in a small fishnet bag and left the house. When she returned later in the evening, she had blades of grass, hay, and clover stuck in her hair, and the smell of the countryside all over her clothes. Niko could not keep his eyes away from his aunt. He saw the laughter deep inside her irises, and happiness like he had never encountered before, shining through her skin and seeping into the objects surrounding her.

Inland

MANOLIS, WHOM POLYCARP NEVER FOUND in his clinic or elsewhere, was inland, having volunteered to work in a makeshift military hospital. He spent his days smelling blood and burnt flesh, hearing the screams of the wounded, many of whom were as young as sixteen. He went from bed to bed, amputating rotten limbs, dressing bullet wounds and limp shreds of flesh converging over deep scarlet holes that would never heal. The dying would grasp at his shoulders or hands, to hold on to dear life. They repeated their own names, for someone to remember them later. Some called their mothers, others their children. There were quiet ones, their eyes fixed on the ceiling, death having already claimed their spirits ahead of their bodies.

He slept little. On those few occasions when he fell into slumber, he dreamt of clean white sheets blowing in the wind, row by row, in the blinding morning sun. This dream, more disturbing than the desolation that surrounded him, awakened him with a racing heart and a tight chest.

The wounded kept coming in truckloads, piled atop the dead, from battlefields that seemed to produce endless supplies of ruined, howling bodies. He did not know where to turn. Thus, he walked in a daze, his stethoscope uselessly dangling from his neck, up and down aisles of groaning, feverish soldiers, some left on the floor until others died, before they could be moved to a bed.

He had been offered the prestigious position of director at the

Greek hospital in Smyrna a few days before the day he had decided to leave the city. It was a position of distinction in the new administration of Smyrna, now run by Greece. The telephone call came to his clinic from the businessman with whom he had run the clandestine operation prior to the occupation. This was followed by a congratulatory letter, which he had spent hours looking at, sitting at his kitchen table. The next morning, dressed in his best suit, he had gone to present his regrets, which nobody understood.

His conscience would not allow it, he said. He explained that his knowledge and expertise lay in treating patients and would thus be put to better use treating the wounded. They took this to be a gesture of self-sacrifice and hailed him as a man of outstanding character and bravery. The truth was that he simply did not want to be in their company, doing their work. After the occupation he gradually came to the realization that Greece had not come there to preserve the world he knew. The people sent hastily to sit in power were unequipped to deal with the Ottoman complexity that had made Smyrna and Western Anatolia so unique over the centuries. He felt betrayed in his hopes, although no promises had been made. He had given his allegiance and taken sides from fear of losing what he cherished. And now he had already lost it, and found the grief intolerable. He realized that the inhabitants of Smyrna were the remnants of an era doomed to disappear. A garden had flourished there on its own, finding the soil fertile, and like all gardens it would suffer inevitable destruction to make way for something new, unfamiliar, and monolithic. He understood now that there was no stopping this eventuality; the fate of Smyrna had been sealed long before anyone understood it.

Thus he threw himself into that no-man's-land called the front, where one's advance caused the other's retreat, and it all boiled down to charred flesh, unrecognizable but for the uniform covering it. Even then, it was not so clear-cut. At times there was Turkish flesh in Austrian uniform and Greek flesh wrapped in British gear. The owners, having usually expired on arrival, could not explain their odd choices of outfits. Megalo Idea and Turkish Nationalism, he mused, clashed on Western Anatolian plains wearing the discarded costumes of outmoded imperial designs.

He had not said goodbye to his friends. He took Katzathoro, his docile and faithful companion, to keep him company and slipped away in the middle of the night, locking doors and shutters. No one knew his whereabouts. He did not have the heart to say goodbye to Elena. He would weep, he felt, for having lacked the courage to declare the love he had carried for so long. If he ever returned, he promised himself as he walked away in the light of a crescent moon, he would take her away from all this.

He doubted he would ever return. Working amidst explosions on a daily basis, he felt it was only a matter of time before he succumbed to death himself, became one of the anonymous cadavers buried daily. In the meantime he tended to whomever he could, tried to save as many as he could, too exhausted to feel fear or hope. Except once. It was an eerily quiet morning. He had finished his rounds in the barracks and had sat down at a makeshift desk used by anyone who had anything to write. Some were reports to be read by some disapproving lieutenant or bespectacled general sitting in the comfort of a drawing room in Athens or Smyrna, sipping Turkish coffee. Most were letters to mothers, lovers, or wives. His went like this:

Elena, my dearest friend,

Perhaps you are wondering where I've been all this time, thinking me rude to have departed in such a hasty manner, without bidding you all a proper goodbye. I am writing this in part to apologize. A few lines only, as sitting down is a luxury I can rarely afford here. I have volunteered to serve as a doctor at the front. I am needed here more than elsewhere; you will be pleased to know that I am not treating only "the rich and flatulent" as you once said, but those once full of life and dreams who are here now waiting to be slaughtered. They are brave, unlike those who sent them here.

He continued writing quickly, once in a while fixing his eyes out of the window as if he were gazing at the scenery, to focus his thoughts. He had to tell her everything, knowing he might never get another chance. It made him free. He was able to speak of things he had withheld since his youth. Such freedom was painful; it hurt him in the chest to be so aware of his impending death and the momentary freedom it afforded him. He made his existence stretch into a lifetime within the few minutes of silence and peace he had managed to find in the barracks. He saw his arm around Elena's waist, feeling her breathe as they took a walk. She turned to him with a smile, her chestnut curls in disarray around her oval face. It was a smile of complicity between lovers, when the beloved is the source of all the joy and happiness in the world. She was giving him the smile he had lived for since he was a little boy. He caressed her cheek. His lips touched her forehead and her eyes, which she closed. He felt her eyelashes tickle his lips as he moved back. He took in the dimple left by her luminous smile on her left cheek. He wanted to pick her up and cradle her in his arms like a baby. He imagined her pregnant. He dreamt it was a time of being forgotten by the rest of the world, of not wanting or knowing anything but the moment itself.

He folded the letter, hands trembling, realizing that the words no longer belonged to him, having left his mind. They were now hers to own and it terrified him to imagine her unfolding the paper and fixing her gaze on his bare soul, somewhere far from her own solitude. He walked over to the box where outgoing mail was placed, threw his envelope on the pile and left the area quickly.

A Few Days Left

ELENA WAS NOT THINKING of Manolis at all as he was writing the missive that tore at his heart. She was standing at the window of her attic, her eyes focused on the cobblestone street to catch a glimpse of Nazım. They had only three days left to spend together. The nights were out of the question, and their days amounted to a few hours here and there, manufactured with the help of lies. A lot of this time together was spent walking or taking rides in carriages that meandered in neighbourhoods where no one knew them. They had developed a routine. She watched him leave his house at the arranged hour, and would follow from a distance until they had turned a few corners, after which they hailed a carriage and sat deep inside so as not to be seen. She would have run away had there been a place to run, to be able to spend that week entirely with him, regardless of consequences. The days fell one by one in their careless punctuality, each sunset imbuing the world with dying colours so that each sunrise that brought her closer to the moment of separation seemed a shade more opaque than the previous.

She gazed at the sky stretched over the rooftops, its black tint washing away to grey with the morning light. Houses, minarets, chimneys, wind roses and the crowns of trees reached towards it, gradually regaining their daylight colours. A rooster sang from one of the yards, the bark of a dog echoed back and forth, and the ezan spread over the reluctant morning sounds from a distant minaret.

He would soon come out of his house, lock the door, and squint at her attic window briefly before walking away. She thought of the day in the fields, among sunflowers and thorns. Lying in the warmth of the sun, cicadas buzzing in her ears, his sweaty golden skin motionless beside hers. It was perhaps in the nature of love itself that each caress, kiss, or gaze amounted to one long goodbye, she pondered. Love's tender cruelty to the heart was its constant reminder of the transience of the body, which it could not do without, while endeavouring to overcome it.

The pale blue door of the townhouse on the other side of the street opened and remained ajar for a few moments. Out came Nazım, his thick dark wavy hair moving out in multiple directions from a small circle at the back of his head. Some of the hair fell over his forehead, sideways, now crossing over one eye as he bent over to make sure he locked the door. He pushed at the locked door in a habitual gesture and used his palm to flatten his hair away from his eyes. He squinted up and saw her gazing down. He acknowledged her with a smile and moved his head sideways before engaging the sidewalk with a light step, shoving his long thin hands into his pockets.

He did not walk like most men, who shuffled their feet a little and moved their hips reluctantly, as if not inclined to move forward. There was a certain bounce to Nazım's gait that made him seem out of place. She wondered if it was the effect of school in Switzerland, with the daily sports activities, or something innate, something that spoke of his being, wanting to sprint forward, away, elsewhere. Even his lovemaking had an acrobatic quality to it, was done zestfully, went somewhere. She wished to fall asleep beside him, in a bed between sheets in another life and told him so later in the carriage taking them towards the villages near the Yamanlar mountains.

"Let's run away to America," she proposed. All she really knew of America was from a few novels, pictures in books, Dvorak's *Symphony of the New World*. She imagined dusty deserts, odd-looking lizards, natives crowned in feathers, bison, and the tall buildings of great cities.

"I have an uncle in San Francisco whom I've never met. His name is Edmund."

He smiled. "We can get off the boat and tell the driver to take us to Edmund, then."

"Well, at least it's a start. I also have some relatives in Marseilles . . . But I heard the rats were as big as cats."

"I have relatives in Ankara," he offered.

"No. I don't know anything about Ankara, besides it's the same country. If you're going to go away, might as well go as far as you possibly can."

"When I go to the front, perhaps you should take your family and go to San Francisco."

"With what money? I just said it like that . . . I'm tired of living like this. Out of one war, into another. That's all. There is nowhere to go."

The mountains looked like green velvet in the mist, as they rode around the outskirts of the city, in and out of sleepy villages. They stopped at a teahouse, where they listened to the story of a man whose village had been burned down during the invasion. Soldiers had raped his bride and left him for dead. She never spoke a word after that, hanging herself in the barn a few days later. The things that my eyes have seen, my heart cannot bear. He swayed as he repeated these words. I live off people's charity. I have no land, no home. My heart cannot bear it. His eyes swam in their cloudy liquid as he spoke, twins looking for a way out of a swamp. We lived like brothers and they've turned us into enemies. He waved his hand vaguely in the air to show them. They came here and tore us apart. I'm a simple man. I work my field and earn my bread. I don't cause anyone any harm. They've torn my life away from me, and who can give it back? I wish they'd killed me instead.

On the way back Nazım stared blankly at the passing scenery. There was a newspaper leaf blowing on the side of the road; racing the carriage, swirling in the wind. There wasn't much time left to spend with Elena now. He regretted his decision, even though he was certain it was the right one. It was a matter of days before the Greek police got to him.

"Eli . . . "

She looked at him and knew.

"I have to leave tomorrow morning."

Elena nodded.

They did not speak until they reached Izmir.

The next morning, Nazım boarded a train headed inland. Elena was gazing down from her attic window as he left his house. He knew. He looked up and touched his lips with one hand, and walked away without looking back. Elena stayed at the window until he disappeared from view. She watched the sky open itself to the sun and the indolent clouds, she stared at a couple of doves engaged in their mating rituals. A man came selling tahan* and pekmez,** two big jugs hanging down from a stick slung across his shoulders, singing "Tahaaan var, pekmez var!" down the street, followed by the vegetable vendor in his horse cart. Women ran out in night-gowns and hair curlers to pick the few vegetables. The bread boy came riding on his bicycle with his frangiola breads. Everyone was going through the motions, pretending things had not changed, even though the vegetables were limp and the bread stale. But it was a day like any other, she observed. It was the same day over and over again, but for indiscernible variations within which entire lives unraveled. The bread boy grew up, his son took up the route, the vegetable man died, another one came, fat ladies and doves went on with their usual routines as men went to war and sons died, daughters got killed, and that was all there was. Life went on. She stood there watching it unfold and yet feeling removed from it. She imagined this exact moment in San Fransisco, which she

* sesame butter
** molasses

had never seen, and in other places she could imagine, happening simultaneously, other faces, different houses and clouds and animals. She had just spent one lifetime at the window and wanted to die suddenly, to lie down and expire, so there would be no further repetition for her.

"What will become of us?" Marie wanted to know. She had just walked in from the neighbour with a few sprigs of parsley, having been treated to a story about the madness of General Hajianestis, the commander of the Greek army.

"In a few months it will all be over," Polycarp said.

Niko walked in, holding an envelope in his hand. "It just came," he said and handed it to his grandmother. The last envelope they had received was years ago; it was the Sultan's condolence letter for Jacob. Letters that came by mail were rarely a good thing. Marie did not reach to take it.

"It is addressed to Elena," said Niko, turning it over in his hands.

"Leave it on the table, we'll tell her when she comes," Marie said with a sigh. Pol took a quick glance.

"This is from Manolis. I recognize the handwriting. At least, we know he's alive."

He sat down, stretched his legs in front of him and closed his eyes. The afternoon sun was already fading behind the lace curtains. The sounds of children came from the empty field where they played. Niko slipped out to join his friends. There would be time for homework later.

"Don't be late!" shouted his uncle, his eyes still closed.

"Shh," retorted the boy, annoyed at having been discovered.

As he skipped down the stairs and towards the street, a group of Greek soldiers walked past. He turned to look, anxious to see where they were going. They stopped in front of Nazım's house and knocked on the door. They knocked louder and louder and finally broke the lock and went inside. Niko felt his limbs turn numb as he continued walking, keeping his head down. He imagined they would drag Nazım out and take him away. He stopped, not knowing if he should go forward or back, legs wobbling. He crouched down, pretending to tie his shoes about five hundred metres from Nazım's house. His hands were trembling. He felt like dashing home but was unable to budge. Neighbours had come to their windows, reluctantly parting lace curtains to watch as the soldiers shouted and made noises, opening and closing doors inside the house. Dear God, dear God, don't let them find him, Niko prayed. He rose and continued walking towards the playing field. He turned around the corner, and watched the scene from afar. The soldiers left the house, empty-handed. Niko sighed with relief. Window curtains fluttered as people moved away from them. As the soldiers marched away Niko got out of his hiding spot and ran home. "Grandma!" he shouted, "Grandma!" She was in the living room with Polycarp, having just witnessed the scene through a parted curtain. The boy threw himself into the old woman's embrace and started sobbing.

"It's all right," she patted his head. "They did not find him. It's all right."

"What if they come tomorrow, or later, and they find him? What if they come here and take us because we were friends with him?"

Marie asked Polycarp where Elena was. Pol did not know, he had not seen her all day.

Elena returned home late and found them sitting quietly in the living room. It was quite dark inside, and it gave her the shivers to see the three silhouettes.

"Ahh!" she cried and froze at the entrance.

Her mother spoke. "Come here. We need to talk."

Elena looked around. "Why aren't the lights on?"

Her mother answered, "Leave them alone and sit down. Where were you?"

Elena sat down slowly, realizing something was wrong. "I was at Clementini's. He is closing his bookshop. I was helping him to pack the boxes."

"What for? Where are we going to get our books now?" said Polycarp, alarmed.

"He's retiring. We'll go to other shops, it isn't the only one. Anyway, are you going to tell me what's wrong or not?"

"They came to take him away!" blurted Niko.

"Who?"

"Greek gendarmes."

"Who did they take away?"

Polycarp explained, "They came to take Nazım away, but he wasn't home. They broke his lock when he did not answer his door. Then they left."

Elena leaned back in the chair.

"We have to warn him so he doesn't go back to his house," Marie said.

"He won't come back," Elena said simply. "He went to the front, joined the army. Gone." She fixed her eyes away from them, feeling that her heart, made of the thinnest glass, had just been crushed.

"What if they come for us? What if they come to question us? Neighbours have seen him come and go to our house."

"We can go to Constantine's for a week," offered Marie.

"Won't it look suspicious that we left the same day they came looking for him?" asked Polycarp.

"What do you propose?" replied Marie.

Niko's teeth started chattering. He tried to hide his trembling hands by sitting on them.

"Let's leave the house tonight, without packing anything. We leave as if we're going for a visit and go to my uncle's. One of us comes around to check during the day, we find out what's happening from the neighbours, and when it's safe we return," offered Elena.

"Will Uncle Constantine want to keep us all at his house?" asked Polycarp.

"We're his family. What kind of a question is that?" scolded

Marie. "I'll go fill a small bag with a change of clothes. You go get your school bag, Niko. Even if we stay at your uncle's, you'll continue to go to school."

Niko was glad to get his school bag for once, since that meant they would leave and be out of danger. He was terrified at the thought of seeing the gendarmes again.

They gathered their coats and left the house when it got dark, having bolted the shutters.

Rescuing Spinoza

WHEN THEY REACHED CONSTANTINE'S HOUSE, Carmela opened the door. She was surprised to see them but motioned them in. Marie explained the reason for their extended visit, and Carmela rushed to make beds for her guests, assuring them they would be safe. Elena rushed after her portly aunt to help with the tasks.

The house would have been spacious if not crammed with large furniture and clutter. There were religious figurines on the wall, and a horseshoe above the door for good luck. Embroidered cushions with Italian proverbs stuffed the sofa and armchairs. A potted plant had been made to climb up the wall and all around the edge of the ceiling. The dining room had a small reproduction of the Last Supper hanging on an otherwise stark wall which had somehow escaped the decorative zeal of Carmela.

Elena looked around the bedroom where Pol and Niko were supposed to sleep. There was a crucifix on the wall over each bed. She had counted the crucifixes all the way to their bedroom and there were nine. "You have so many crucifixes, Auntie!" she observed out loud, "Where did you find them all?" Carmela, not catching the amused tone in her query, replied, "Father Francisco was renovating his quarters—he got new ones and I took his old ones. I have a few more, but I have no more room to put them." Elena nodded. "Do Father Fransisco's new crucifixes look very different now?"

"They're bigger, more vivid. Do you need some?"

"No," said Elena and fluffed the pillow in its pillowcase. "Thank you for taking us in, Auntie. We were quite afraid."

"The least we could do," Carmela responded, shaking her curly head. It occurred to Elena that her aunt's crucifix obsession and her being childless might be related somehow, and she felt sad at the thought.

Uncle Constantine would be working late at the tavern. She wasn't working today, felt too tired, Carmela said. Elena knew that after their fights, as a rule, she refused to go to the tavern and left him alone to do all the tasks, until he crawled back to her, apologizing and begging. Since Elena and Niko had stopped going to the tavern, he probably needed his wife to be there more than ever.

"He needs to hire someone to help him there. I can't handle standing so long at the stove frying sardines. My feet get swollen and they hurt for days. I'm getting old and tired."

"Nobody can make sardines like you do," Elena said as they left the room. "His customers will miss you too much."

Her aunt smiled feebly and shrugged. "Not so many customers any more. People don't feel cheerful enough to go out. They don't have money. I tell him it's the right time to sell the tavern, get rid of it, so we don't grow old in poverty. But he won't listen. 'What will I do,' he says? 'What will I do? Crochet doilies and knit sweaters with you?'" She chuckled.

They went to bed in fresh white sheets that night, and felt rested being away from home. Elena lay awake thinking of Nazım, whether he was still alive.

She thought of the painting of Dulle Griet which she had almost finished and needed to deliver to Van der Meer. Perhaps he would have news of Nazım. She thought of the day in Clasomeni, where they made love in the fields. It was crawling with bugs unaware there was a war going on. There was an entire world of creatures in Smyrna who were oblivious to it. The thought comforted her and she fell asleep.

Niko dozed suddenly that night. He had planned to tell his grandmother he would continue to stay here from now on, as he was terrified of the soldiers. His uncle's cellar was not half as fearsome.

Maria knelt in front of the crucifix and prayed for her family's safety and the souls of the departed. She spoke to Jacob in her mind, the way she did every night. As she fell asleep she realized they had forgotten to tell Elena about Manolis's letter.

The next day Pol, who had lain awake all night, shuffled off to their house to retrieve the letter and see if anything had changed. He took the long route, on his way back, in order not to be noticed. He thought of the hat store and how the demand for hats had trickled to practically nothing as the war raged on. The confrontation between Kemal's army and the Greeks was closer to Izmir than before, the Greek army having consistently retreated west. Beggars seemed to be everywhere. The city had gone into a state of melancholy quietude. It had also gotten dirty, with paper and dirt blowing and swirling about on the sidewalks.

He likened the city to a widow left alone in a large house where her children's shrieks and husband's laughter once bounced off the walls, where everything spoke of liveliness. The widow now sat looking at the mute walls, its paint coming off here and there, furniture creaking joylessly, the musty, dusty smell of old age coming off her body and the house, death waiting around the corner. This was Smyrna now.

Their house appeared intact. He went in, took the envelope from the table, inhaling the unique smell inside, somewhat woody and spicy, with a whiff of turpentine. He climbed up the stairs to the attic to see Elena's painting. It looked finished. He supposed she needed to add a few touch-ups that only she would notice. He made a mental note to tell her about it. The sooner the painting left the house, the better. There was something ominous about it. He went to his room to pick up a book and remembered that they had forgotten Spinoza in the house. He rushed quickly to the kitchen, where he found Spinoza dozing under the cover over his cage. He took the cover off, opened the cage and let the bird fly out. He delicately removed the little water cup and changed the water, added some seeds. He changed the newspaper lining and lifted his finger for the bird to return. A few minutes later, he left the house, taking Spinoza and Elena's letter with him.

Aunt Carmela had prepared lentil soup. She was humming "La Paloma" as she busied herself setting the table. The arrival of her husband's family seemed to have injected a cheerful mood in her that was contagious. Everyone was smiling without quite knowing why. Marie looked dried-up and old compared to her sister-in-law, whose smooth white skin had formed no wrinkles around her eyes and mouth. As she moved, one could hear her stockinged thighs rub against each other.

It was noon. Niko had returned from school and they were waiting for Constantine. When he walked into the fragrant kitchen, placing his hat on the rack in a habitual gesture, Carmela observed that her husband's eyes were mellow with joy. For once they had a full house, a family, and they were pleased. She called everyone to the table, and soup was served, steaming from the plates. Carmela stretched open her thick soft arms and said "Bon apétit!" and the clinking of spoons took over.

Elena was intrigued by the envelope that sat in her dress pocket. She finished her soup quickly and excused herself to go to the bathroom to read Manolis's letter. She ripped the letter from its envelope and opened it. Her eyes focused on the middle part of the letter.

It seemed before I never found the time to tell you the things that mattered most. Now, I realize I simply lacked the courage. Ever since I came here, two things have preoccupied me: the possibility that I may die at any moment, and my intense desire to return to your side. I need you to know that you have been my only great inspiration in life, that I have loved you from the deepest, most genuine part of my being as long as I can remember. I have done everything I could to be in your vicinity. Sitting where I am now, with death breathing on me, it is easy to say this: I cannot utter your name without aching to see you, or see you without hurting to reach you. Elena, you are my prayer.

She read it again and again, recalling the boy who had always followed her like a shadow, who used his own sleeve to wipe her nose when she cried and offered her dandelions and rocks in that distant time called childhood. She remembered all those moments she had taken for granted, which spoke of his affection, and her eyes filled up for her friend who saw death in the face now. She thought of the unfairness of life, how sometimes one nurses a love that swells and curls within the heart, but is claimed by no one.

If I return from this hellish place and find you waiting, I long to take you by the hand to a faraway world, uncorrupted by our nightmares. You may not love me. But I hope you will be there for me to love.

Yours always,

She folded the page on which her tears had already smudged the ink and placed it in her pocket, taking out a handkerchief to blow her nose. Realizing this was Nazım's made her weep even more, so that the piece of cloth was drenched in tears as she stuffed it back into her pocket. She washed her face before leaving the confines of the small bathroom.

Halkapınar Station

AFTER HE HAD DISAPPEARED from Elena's field of vision up in the attic that smelled of turpentine and oils, Nazım took the tramway to the Halkapınar Station. It was a one-storey, grey building with arched windows in the Greco-Turkish style of the nineteenth century and looked like any other stop in the web of train stations that spread across Anatolia. Its European counterparts, he recalled, rose like churches even in the most insignificant cities, with tall arched ceilings and overlooking marble spaces that gleamed in the filtered light of cathedral windows, immense clocks, and brass trimmings that shone with efficiency. Not here. You are not encouraged to go anywhere, and if you must come, you are not expected to stand around looking at ceilings and walls. There was a small ticket booth in one corner, housing a jaundiced bureaucrat more interested in sipping his tea than selling tickets. In another corner was a clock, placed haphazardly, with a pendulum that swung indolently and couldn't possibly tell the correct time. Blinding sunlight squeezed through every crack and flooded the space from the easterly windows, falling upon the travellers in the serpentine queue in front of the ticket booth, adding to their discomfort. He thought of Elena's brother, forced to board a train here in his underwear, bound for eastern Anatolia, disappearing into its arid landscape, never to be heard of again. He wondered if a similar fate awaited him. If he stayed, the Greeks would surely torture and kill him. They had already singled him out as one of the locals who shot at Greek soldiers on the Quay on the day of the occupation. If he managed to reach the front, he would probably die from a bullet.

Or perhaps not. Perhaps he would survive and return to a new order, a republic, new civility . . . He imagined Elena sailing towards him like a white boat on the turquoise waters of the Aegean. Or she would be a rotting corpse buried somewhere, unfound. And he would spend the rest of his life mourning the day he left her standing in her attic window holding a brush. She wore a navy blue dress with a lace trim around the neck. Her curly chestnut hair surrounded her face somewhat seditiously with eyes like magnets pulling him back, so that every step forward was an effort of will.

He looked around furtively for any Greek soldiers; he did not see any. The queue was advancing slowly. The man in front of him had a sun-baked face and wore a bright yellow embroidered headcloth. He probably came from a village and smelled of mud and wool. Nazım cherished the smell; it assured him he was home and among the people of his land. There weren't any fezzes, he remarked. He was wearing a bowler hat himself.

The night before, he had visited Van der Meer, his only friend. The tall blond Dutchman had connections that provided intelligence to which few had access in Izmir. He had assured Nazım that Kemal's army had made gains in Anatolia and the Greek army was in disarray. General Hajianestis, it appeared, had pretty much lost his mind. He assured Nazım that the liberation would not be long and he was confident they would meet again.

"And you?" Nazım asked.

"I'll make sure your sister is safe. I'll send her off if things get dangerous. Your painter friend too. When she comes to deliver my painting, I'll offer to take her family away, wherever they want to go."

Nazım insisted, "What about you?"

"What about me, my dear man? I will pack my little suitcase and hide in my closet until it's all over, what else?" He laughed.

"Maybe I'll move to Holland and distribute Marxist pamphlets on the street."

Nazım looked serious.

"Listen," Van der Meer continued, "you have a mission. You want to fight the war, build a country, go to the villages . . . I have my father's boats, my Swiss education and Dutch name. What do you want me to do? I have already done my part. There isn't much else . . . and don't tell me the revolution is for everyone, and that everyone is equal in it. Once all the dust settles, there is always a regime, and it thirsts for an enemy. It happens every time. The difference between you and me is that you want to set things right, while I merely want to get rid of the wrong."

When he finally boarded the train and felt it pull slowly out of the station he took a deep breath. He was still not out of danger as there were random checkpoints along the way. Afyon was his destination, where Kemal's army had established itself, pushing the weakened Greek forces further west. He did not think the train would take him that far, and had resolved to walk part of the way through mountains and friendly villages. He stared out the window as the train advanced towards the countryside. The love of one's country, he mused, was meaningless if it wasn't about the smell of mud and wool at a train station, and the toothless dark-faced man across from him with wrinkles running across his face like well-beaten dirt roads on which so much life had travelled, and the grandchild on his knee, and the olive trees and immense skies that filled the window of his wagon. The woman who holds your heart. It meant all these things, kneaded in sunlight and misery this very day, from which he felt he could never part. It was not about abstractions. A place on earth could claim one's soul, the way a mother claims her young. It is the earth that claims us, yet we fight to claim it. He thought of Van der Meer's words with unease. Whose country would it be once the empire and the vultures were gone? Who would decide? Why was Elena's brother taken away merely for his name?

He thought about his comforting dream of communism; it worked for the Russians, would it work for us, he repeated to himself. His thoughts were interrupted with visions of his sister as a child with rosy cheeks. Back then, he did not even know she was his sister. His father's love child, with eyes like olives. The sibling for whom he would like to change the world. He felt a sob rise to his throat. Grieving for his own naïve notions, the small hurting child inside who believed in good would redeem all that had been lost.

The wrinkled peasant took two hard-boiled eggs out of a kerchief after carefully undoing the knots. His joints were swollen and red. His granddaughter sat next to him in a state of sedate boredom, looking around at other passengers and occasionally picking her nose. The old man slowly peeled one egg and offered it to the child who started nibbling at it, holding it with both hands. He then peeled the other and offered it to Nazım, who politely refused and looked out the window.

"You take it, son," said the old man. "You need it more than I do."

"No thanks, uncle. I just ate before boarding the train."

The old man stared at him for a long while. "You are not only skinny but a bad liar too." He proceeded to tear a loaf of bread. The girl took one piece and started chewing hungrily. The old man carefully tore another piece.

"Take the egg, I said," he insisted and lowered his voice, "you can't fight a war on an empty stomach. I'd give you more, but that's all I have."

Nazım reluctantly took the egg, thanking the man, and proceeded to eat it absentmindedly.

"Why are you dressed this way?" asked the old man. "That hat and suit, the shiny shoes . . . " There was scorn in his tone.

"That is all I have," muttered Nazım, who felt exposed. The old man leaned over, whispering, "If the Greeks check the train, they'll know what you're up to before they ask. You look like a boy from the city looking for the wrong army, child . . . it's written on the shiny shoes and the infidel hat. Do you speak Greek?"

"A little," Nazım replied.

"That won't do. You can't even pretend you're one of them."

Nazım felt desperate. "What can I do? It's too late . . . "

"Here," said the old man, undoing the yellow kerchief on his head, "you put it on."

Nazım took the kerchief, which smelled of oily hair and cows, unable to hide his repulsion.

"You want to live, city boy?" the old man asked, observing Nazım carefully as he tried to wrap the kerchief around his head. "You don't even know how to do this!"

The old man rose to wrap it for him.

"Now dirty your shoes, make them dusty. No peasant walks around with shiny leather shoes in these parts."

Nazım took off his shoes and started rubbing them face down on the floor until they looked scratched and dusty.

"They still look new . . . " the old man said, shaking his head. "Step on the back of the shoe with your heel, like a slipper."

Nazım tried to push in the backs of the shoes by standing on them, wondering how he would manage to walk in them later.

"Take off the tie. Dirty your jacket. Tear it a little and try to make your face look a little grubbier. You're the colour of verdigris. A peasant looks healthy, not like you. Well, you can always pretend you have consumption . . . Judging from your colour you probably have it anyway."

The old man was sizing him up, as Nazım tried to follow his instructions.

"What do they call you?"

"Nazım."

"Hmm . . . You can't talk like a book, city boy. Try to speak like me."

"I don't know how!"

"Suit yourself."

The old man tied up the empty kerchief on his lap and brushed off the bread crumbs. His granddaughter nodded off, as she leaned on his arm. He leaned on the window and closed his eyes.

Nazım got up, dragging his shoes to the bathroom, wary of Greek gendarmes. How long can I keep this up, he wondered, as he opened the door to the narrow toilet. He could see the train tracks speeding underneath, making shrill noises as the wheels pressed upon them. He felt nauseous and dizzy standing there, but temporarily safe. He knew it was best to get off the train as soon as possible. He had better chances of surviving if he went the rest of the way on foot. Perhaps the old peasant would help him. This thought gave him new courage and he decided to wait in the bathroom until the next station. I wonder where the old man will get off. The train blew its long whining whistle as it sped along rhythmically. He loved this sound. Because it reminds me of my loneliness. Solitude was the theme of his life, ever since he was a child, except for the few years when he could play with Despina, before she became his sister. He thought of the massive dark brown furniture, marble-topped tables, and oversized mirrors in the living room that had made him feel crushed and small. The silence of the house. His mother shuffling back and forth quietly, cooking and working. Never sang to herself. His father, the pasha, with the elaborate costume which made him look invincible, fearsome. The softness of bulging flesh, the delicacy of a wrinkle, the truth of a hairy forearm—his father had none of these. From the neck down he was made of cardboard or steel, something unforgiving, in any case. His grey moustache curled with a hint of brown at the edges. Even in that, he could not find humanity as a child; it was perfectly groomed. Nazım realized in the speeding washroom that he had never seen his father undressed. Not even when he was dead. At that point, he merely became a cold, leathery pasha in the everlasting stiff uniform.

As the train slowed down, he opened the door a crack and slipped out to see the old man. Perhaps they could leave the train together. He might let him carry his granddaughter. He entered the wagon where the old peasant was sitting. He was about to put on his jacket. Nazım cleared his throat. "Uncle, do you think I can get off with you? Maybe you'd let me hold the child in my arms? I can't see how else I'll make it to the front."

The old man became pensive, took one look out the window. "Hurry then. Take her and let's go."

They climbed down the steps, Nazım holding the child in front of his face, hoping the headscarf would hide part of his profile. The old man was beside him, carrying a battered suitcase held together with ropes. He pointed his finger towards the station door. Nazım nodded and they moved as swiftly as they could, passing in front of the Greek gendarmes who gazed over everyone's head. Nazım was counting his steps under his breath,

"One, two, three, . . . fifteen . . . twenty-five . . . " The door to freedom was approaching.

"Please God don't let them get me now," he prayed.

They stepped out of the station. He took a deep breath, squinting around at the world bathed in sunlight. The old man pulled his sleeve towards a horse cart on which an old woman sat in peasant garb. They got on. The old man whispered something to the woman and they set off, wheels creaking.

On the Plains of Anatolia

THEY ARRIVED IN THE VILLAGE, and the horse cart climbed up the hill towards a small house surrounded by young poplars swaying in the morning breeze. Their dainty leaves shimmered in the light like thousands of tiny green mirrors.

"This is her dowry," said the old man looking from the trees to the girl. She was his only grandchild, orphaned during the war. Her name was Gül. He said that it was the custom in these parts that you planted poplars when a girl was born and you sold the wood to marry her off. The old woman stopped the horse in the shade of the trees.

"Who were these for?" Nazım asked, pointing at the older poplars that were also there.

There was one daughter who died at the age of three from a fever, another one who eloped with a Rum from a neighbouring village at the age of fifteen. She never returned, a good thing too, muttered the old man. His wife's face remained impassive.

"She is now in Rhodes, I hear," continued Halit. "Has three children. All infidels. The devil take them all."

The woman frowned, but said nothing.

Nazım changed the subject, not wanting to utter an opinion that would upset his host. "What a lovely view from up here," he said as he looked around at the the mountains and plains surrounding the hill.

"I'll make you something to eat," announced the woman heavily as she entered the house. The little girl had woken up and ran after her grandmother into the house. Her grandmother instructed her to feed the horse, and she seemed to know exactly what to do as she hurried towards the barn. Nazım needed to know where he was and how to get to Afyon on foot. Halit explained that they were in the mountains of Manisa and it would take him a few days to get to Afyon through the mountains, if he walked. He needed to know which villages to avoid and which to go through.

"We need to give you clothes first, villagers here all look the same, at least you won't stand out."

He rose from the straw stool and walked into the house, trying to straighten his back.

"Woman! Woman, give this boy some clean clothes to wear, will you?"

Nazım felt uneasy as he heard the woman mumbling in the background.

Halit responded to her curtly, "Your son isn't coming back. Give the boy his clothes."

Nazım heard a pot being slammed and more mumbling from the woman.

"Fine, I'll do it!" said the man. A few minutes later he came out with the clothing in his arms.

"I've given you both so much trouble already. I don't want to upset Aunt. Maybe I should just start walking if you show me the direction . . . "

Nazım got up, and Halit was upset. "City boy, do you want to fight this war or die on the way? The wife has been on my case the last fifteen years, it has nothing to do with you. Put these on. There . . . go in that way and close the door. Tell me if they fit."

He waved his hand to show Nazım where to go.

Nazım obeyed the old man and walked into the house, coming face to face with the old woman.

"I'm so sorry," he said and extended the clothes, "here, I don't need them."

The old woman stared him in the eyes. "Don't be a fool and do what the man says. My boy is dead, he isn't coming back. Maybe his clothes will bring you luck." She spoke sullenly and went back to chopping onions, tears streaming down her eyes.

As Nazım put on the baggy pants and the wide kerchief around his waist, he wondered whether the clothes would bring him luck, or take away whatever was left of it. He felt anxiety knowing they belonged to a dead man, but tried to shrug off the superstition. His beard had started to grow. He needed a cap. He came out of the small room, bending his head so as not to hit the doorway. Halit was waiting for him. His face fell and he looked away seeking composure.

"Vay, vay! They look as though they were sewn for you." He smiled showing a gap in his teeth. "Do you mind if I call you Memo?"

Nazım was taken aback, he hesitated.

"It's a better name for you now. Forget the old one. It's for city folk. This one's just right."

His dialect had become thicker.

"So be it, then," said Nazım and smiled nervously.

"Woman, come see Memo!"

The old woman rushed out wiping her hands, her face a mixture of hope and disbelief.

Nazım saw the woman reel. She swayed a bit and leaned on the wall, wilting. He could see the whites of her eyes. She quietly slipped to the ground and crouched into a fetal position before keeling over. Her body started trembling violently.

The old man shuffled indoors shouting, "Hold her head on your lap!"

He returned with a piece of wood which he proceeded to put between her teeth. She twitched like a fish on a boat for what seemed an eternity. Finally, her muscles relaxed and she seemed to have fallen asleep. The two men carried her to the sofa that stood in front of the house and laid her there.

"She's always had this," Halit said as he covered her with a light blanket. "Come, the soup must be ready."

He walked in and stirred the pot, calling out to his granddaughter, who was playing with a kitten further away in the meadow. She rose slowly, holding a piece of string that the kitten leaped to catch. Each time the kitten fell back the girl would give a high-pitched giggle. When she finally arrived, her grandfather told her to set the table.

The old woman lay on the sofa while they ate. Occasionally she would lift her eyelids and look around. Gül drank her soup from the bowl without bothering with her spoon and rushed to sit next to her grandmother. Caressing her head for a while, slowly she lay beside her with her arm hanging limply around her waist and fell asleep embracing her. Halit shook his head. "What will this child do if we die? We both have one foot in the grave already. No other family . . . God willing one of us will live long enough to marry her off."

Nazım shook his head in sympathy. He felt drained suddenly, realizing he had been making great efforts ever since he boarded the train in the station. First to survive, and now to adjust to his new identity as a peasant named Memo. He watched the old woman and the girl sleeping in their embrace, wishing he could sleep the next few months off, wake up and find Elena waiting for him so they could take the boat to wherever it was she wished to go. San Francisco. The other side of the world, where they had a Mediterranean climate and spoke American English. He didn't know much about the place except that it was a port and ships would enter and depart blowing their long melancholy horns, as seagulls flew above . . . He fell into a reverie.

Halit cleaned up the table and disappeared. His wife and the child were sleeping peacefully. Nazım was sitting at the table, disoriented. I am a fake peasant about to cross the mountains and go to war, he remembered. Beyond all that floated the slim possibility of survival, and the even more nebulous chance that he would serve in the east, among people he did not know, to help build a new nation. There were no blue velvet trimmings or milky hands in that future. No Elena whose curls tickled his nostrils and whose hips snuggled against his on a ship. Nazım realized he did not know how to run away. It required talents he did not have. He felt forlorn, a stranger to himself, wearing a dead man's clothes, submitting to the old man's longing gaze for his dead son.

He rose from the chair and looked in the distance, towards the horizon. The afternoon sun was beating down on the plains, making the earth steam. I should get going, he thought. He peeked into the house to find old Halit sleeping on a cot near the small kitchen, his knees raised to his chest and a tespih hanging from his loose fingers. Nazım touched his shoulder. "Uncle! Uncle! I'll get going now . . . "

The old man opened his eyes and stared ahead blankly. Slowly he sat up and focused on Nazım.

"Don't you want to stay a while?"

Nazım shook his head. "I've imposed on your family enough. It's time for me to go."

The old man shook his head sadly. "I see. I thought you might help me with the field a little, seeing that my hands hurt and the wife is so sick . . . Just a few days, not long, if you could spare . . ." He gazed at Nazım hopefully.

"If you need my help, I will stay," Nazım replied, feeling lighter as he uttered these words. The prospect of walking though mountains and forests without a map and in ruined shoes was daunting.

Halit rose from the cot, holding his waist. "It creaks," he smiled as he tried to straighten up. "I'll show you the fields."

They walked downhill towards the meadows.

Days followed one after another and Nazım lost track of time in the company of Halit and his family. He learned the art of picking vegetables, with a kerchief tied around his waist to form a pouch. His hands became calloused. It was tedious labour, each day he would pick two to three loads of bamyas, two-meals worth. His dreams of farming with Elena by his side began to seem unrealistic.

He also started teaching the child how to read. The girl had a very limited vocabulary, since she did not meet many people. No one ever came to visit. Halit occasionally took her to town where he sold vegetables and bought what he needed at home, and that was the extent of her social contact. She spoke very occasionally and only when it was urgent or necessary to do so. Nazım began to see his tutoring of her as his small contribution to the social renewal he had dreamt of in another life, thus threading together his old life and the new into something that had more meaning than running away or even joining an army to which he did not feel he had anything of value to contribute except his flesh.

Retreat

NOT FAR FROM WHERE NAZIM took refuge, less than a hundred kilometres away, Manolis was packing his medical equipment and his few belongings, having got word that they were to retreat further west. This was reportedly a tactical move, to get the army closer to Smyrna and its surrounding regions, where the infrastructure would help them defend their position. To Manolis, who had seen soldiers die in great numbers on a daily basis, this was a euphemism for defeat. As Kemal's army made gains, the Greek inhabitants of the region burned their villages and houses to leave no spoils behind as they fled ahead of their army. Manolis wondered how Smyrna would look under the onslaught of panicked villagers and peasants seeking refuge.

His own personal retreat had begun recently, at the precise moment when Katzathoro, his faithful companion, died, hit by a stray bullet. Or a bullet that could have killed a soldier instead. He had stroked the dog's head and ears as he breathed his last shallow breath, looking at Manolis with his large brown eyes that suddenly froze. He buried the dog and shed no tears, rushing back to tend the wounded and the dying men. That night during one of his short fitful naps he awoke, startled, with a sob that rolled through his body like a giant wave. It took him along in its violent tumble; with him were all the eyes whose gaze had gone out like Katzathoro's. When it crashed, he was left breathless, his face in the pillow, his body shaking, his fists punching the silent white mound. When it passed, he sat on his cot, holding his face in his hands. I cannot do this anymore. I'd rather die. I'd rather die.

Outside, he heard the sirens, there had been another raid, more bombings. He heard the wheels of the ambulance screeching to a halt. He knew the sounds by heart. He could piece them together and tell the story of what had happened. He thought he could even hear the thud of blood pumping out of a missing leg before he tended to it in the ambulance. He could hear the wheeze of organs ripped open by a bullet, the hissing of gaps that would never mend, the metal stuck in the brain, the almost imperceptible jerking of a man's limbs a few seconds after he died. They were almost all children, some barely seventeen, with long eyelashes and healthy cheeks still padded with baby fat, guts filled with unforgiving bullets, crying for their mothers. He loathed himself for his past beliefs, for having absurdly wanted to preserve his world, for having gone to such great lengths to smuggle all this metal that now came back to haunt him, lodged inside pieces of mangled flesh. To fulfill his oath. Lately he felt relieved when they died, their souls released, unlike his that was trapped in the midst of all this horror. He no longer wished for an end to the war. He no longer wished to return to the past. He simply wanted an end to living.

He rose slowly and walked out of his sleeping quarters. He walked through the field, past the ambulance where the driver was waiting to open the door to the back for him. He walked past the man who was talking to him, past the moaning, and the stench of corpses coming from the freshly dug graves. He walked, with his stethoscope dangling in front of him and his eyes unfocused, towards where the gunfight continued to rage. He took off his white jacket that was bloodstained and threw it on the ground. The noises ceased. He walked past a silent walnut tree. He tore the stethoscope off his neck and threw it down. People were gesticulating, waving at him to come back. Someone started running to catch him.

When the soldier tried to hold him back, Manolis punched him and continued walking. With each step he left his burdened life farther and farther behind. He felt free at last. He remembered Elena at her window when she flicked the coin at him. He smiled. Then the world hid itself behind a black curtain.

He was told that days went by before he opened his eyes again. Exhaustion, they called it. You were walking straight into the line of fire. What were you thinking? He could not say. You punched a guy who tried to stop you. He lost his front teeth. You walked a few hundred meters and collapsed. We thought you were shot. He did not want to hear the story. He had tried to make his life disappear, but it had returned, in the halting words of a corporal. Do you remember any of it?

A week later they sent him to Smyrna; extended sick leave, they called it. They gave him a medal too, for his heroic efforts. At the station, he threw the medal on the tracks before boarding the train to Halkapınar. He had spoken few words since the incident; like a man who suffers from an inflamed throat, he tried to economize on sounds, making the least possible effort. He was wearing the same coat he wore when he first travelled to the front, except that now it looked like a hand-me-down from a heftier man, someone with greater stature.

The train was full, people standing wherever they could. Manolis found a corner in the hallway by a window where he could stand and look outside. The smell of bodies was overpowering. He tried to open the window for a while, before noticing that the handle was broken. He had not shaved in a long time, a dark beard covered most of his face. His own reflection in the mirror made his pulse quicken with anxiety. He was still there. It was still he. He looked around at the people around him. Some were wounded soldiers; damaged goods shipped home. There were women and children, either going to visit relatives or returning after a visit. Perhaps they were simply running away from the war.

He turned his back to the crowd, pressing his face to the window. If he looked out he would not faint, he thought. He tried to take his mind elsewhere. He imagined the turquoise sea, a beach, crabs crawling about sideways, the softness of driftwood. The train heaved and started moving. Pushing people against each other before they straightened up. Life took off from the station with suitcases, bags, jackets, hats, bandages. He did not know what he would do in Smyrna, except hide in his house. Pretend he wasn't there. Pretend he wasn't himself. He did not need to pretend, for he was not. He would try to move on. An Aegean island, perhaps, where no one knew him. They would leave him alone. He would liquidate his assets, his parents' vineyard, his grandmother's house, the land in Thrace, and build a small house by the sea. Chios? Samos? Farther? He would never have to be a doctor again. He did not want to run into Elena. What if they saw him? The letter. He felt his anxiety crawl from his fingertips up to his chest, onto the heart; a couple of spiders surrounding the centre of him with their sticky webs, squeezing.

A man whose bandaged head had bled into the white gauze stood across from him, grinning. Manolis did not recognize him. He looked away, wondering if he had bandaged that head, if there was a story to be remembered. Nothing came to mind. He looked at the man again. This time the man smiled with an open mouth. Front teeth missing. Ah! Sensing some recognition in him, the man tried to squeeze his way towards Manolis. Great. He's coming to talk to me, the toothless man with a hurting head. He's pushing the crowd around to speak to me. The man finally reached him. "Do you remember me?"

Manolis shook his head no and looked away, hoping to discourage further conversation.

"Are you sure?" insisted the man, still grinning.

"Did I have anything to do with the bandage?" Manolis gave in.

"No. You had something to do with my missing teeth."

"Ah! Sorry."

"You threw the stethoscope down and kept walking. I came to

stop you, a few more metres and you would have been shot. Then you punched me in the face. The nose was bruised too, but got better. It's just the teeth. I tried to find them on the ground. They said you could stick them right back in. I must have swallowed them, though. Never found them . . . " He grinned. "You've become a good boxer, Manolis."

It irked Manolis to hear his name spoken by a soldier. No one ever addressed him by his first name.

"How do you know my name?" He was upset.

"You don't recognize me, do you?"

"No."

"Your father owned a vineyard in Focia. Made retzina."

Manolis kept staring at the toothless man, trying to remember him.

"Mine was a psaras," the man went on. "Fisherman. We lived next door to you."

"Oh my God, are you snotty Yanni?"

"Hey, you were the one who peed in his pants during class, Doctor!"

"Why did you never talk to me before?"

Yanni shrugged. "You were so busy all the time, and a doctor. Such an important man . . . "

"Did I do that too?" He pointed at his bandaged head. "No. That was a bullet. Still in there. I'm going back to Focia. You?"

"Don't know. Smyrna, I guess."

He started feeling nauseated, remembering bullets, organs, despair.

"Are you feeling ill?"

"A little . . . " He wanted a different subject, fast. "So, are you married, kids, single? Tell me. I left Focia such a long time ago . . . "

"Yes, married, three kids, with a fourth one on the way. My father died while I was away, they wrote me. The fourth one is due next month. I suppose I'll go back to fishing now."

"You might want to leave, Yanni. Greece is losing the war here. Put your family on the boat and go somewhere else."

"You think?" Yanni became thoughtful. "Where would I go? Home is here . . . I was born here . . . "

"You're a fisherman, my friend. As long as you have a boat, you'll find fish!"

Yanni shook his head. "My wife, she's Turkish . . . We belong here."

"If you say so," replied Manolis.

Yanni had lost his cheer and looked depressed. Manolis wondered what would happen to him, a doomed family man divided in identity, his children falling through the cracks. A little later Yanni touched his shoulder. Reluctantly, Manolis turned his eyes towards him.

"Mano, I am afraid for my family . . . " Yanni's hands were trembling. "What if they are dead?" Tears came to his eyes. "What if they raped her? Skewered my babies? I have seen it happen, Mano. I have seen it happen . . . " He broke down and started sobbing, wiping his face with his sleeve. He leaned his face on Manolis, muffling his sobs on his coat. Manolis put his arm around the man's back. He did not know what to do. "Shh . . . Shhh . . . " There was nothing he could say. Indeed, they might all have been skewered by either group. A definite possibility and not easily dismissed. "Calm down, Yanni. Calm down . . . Come, let's look out the window for a bit." The devastated man nodded and leaned his forehead on the window, with his eyes closed. "Listen," whispered Manolis, "for all you know, they might all be safe and sound, waiting for your return. Do not despair like this. Be strong. Hope for the best."

Yanni became calmer, and Manolis returned to his own ruminations. Samos? Crete? Crete was far enough. Perhaps there. Elena? Would she go with him? How could he face her now, in this state of moral defeat? Elena, here I am. My soul is the colour of charcoal. I dream of torn flesh and bullets every night. Dead eyes haunt my days. I am adrift in nothingness. Will you marry me? Sure.

The train slowed down as it entered Halkapınar Station. The crowd in the wagon became restless as if on cue, looking for bags, jackets, children, money, and finally pushed past each other towards the door. Manolis felt his heart sink. Being on the train was good. Time was suspended, it did not belong anywhere in particular. As soon as the train stopped life took over once again. There was some place to go, something to do with all those minutes and hours. Manolis watched the people, rushing off the train, hauling bags and children. Yanni was still standing by the wagon window, reluctant to leave. Manolis looked at him. "Snotty Yanni," he forced a smile, "time to get off." Yanni simply nodded and they started walking together slowly toward the exit.

Inside the station, they stood facing each other. "Best of luck, Yanni. May you find everyone safe and sound," Manolis said, opening his arms. Yanni had extended a trembling hand which he then put aside and hugged Manolis. "You find them, and you take them away from here, you hear?" whispered Manolis. He dipped his hand into his pocket and came up with some crumpled bills. "I don't need this. You take it, for your kids. Good luck." He squeezed the money into Yanni's hand and walked away. He had forgotten how noise enveloped one here. Vendors, porters, horse carriages, all rushing about.

He walked towards the Quay, his thoughts lingering on Yanni as he advanced in the direction of the sea. There were women everywhere, walking, smiling, moving their curly heads in stylish hats, waists tightened by corsets, parasols over their heads, the breeze playfully lifting and playing with their white chiffon dresses. Blue sea and sailboats in the background, children running about in pinafores. The familiar pot-pot-pot of a fishing boat approaching the coast. He remembered afternoon slumbers here, listening to that hypnotic sound in another life, long ago. He blinked, perhaps he was hallucinating. He looked at his hands and dusty shoes. He remembered he was unshaven; his head, a ball of unwashed hair with two holes for eyes. He looked like a beggar, one of those veterans from the great war who had dotted the streets of Smyrna a few years ago.

He backed towards a building to obtain shade, leaning on the limestone wall, holding his crumpled hat with both hands. Out of sight. He felt like a stain in the landscape, a premonition of things to come. A group of women with children walked away. He remained in the shade, gazing at the bay across the street, the open skies. A streetcar pulled by horses in straw hats interrupted his gaze. He started walking alongside the wall, quickening his pace. He wanted to think his plan through. There was probably no time to sell his house or land, he realized. He remembered his clinic and patients in Kemeraltı. He had to get rid of that too. The nausea returned.

His mind clung to the vision of the women and their parasols. There were plans he was trying to make, and thoughts he could not successfully string together; and there was this image offering refuge, some kind of vague hope, a desire for a future that could contain such vaporous levity as was around him. It appeared so uncorrupted and simple. A year or two ago, he would not have noticed it, taking it for granted. I have paid for this yearning with my innocence. He walked beside the building with a broken heart, like a starving man brought to his knees at the sight of fresh bread in a bakery window.

He arrived at his house. It looked intact. He pushed open the heavy door with its cast-iron leafy decoration and entered the house. It smelled of abandoned furniture. This is how furniture behaves when you are gone, he thought. The tables and beds and chairs absorb your odours, then release them in their concentrated, stifling essence once you're gone. He walked through the dark house, from room to empty room, like a burglar searching. He opened the blinds in his bedroom and flung open the windows, noticing the large cushion on the floor on which Katzathoro used to curl up to sleep. It still had his hair, and the imprint of his curled-up body. He quickly walked through the house, pulling back curtains and opening windows, letting sunlight and fresh air fill the house. Then he sat still at his favourite kitchen chair, looking around in the midst of the silence. The house revealed nothing to him. He got up and walked back to his bedroom, where he flung himself on the covers without removing his shoes and stared at the ceiling. He no longer knew where to go, what plans to make. He heard the shrieks of playing children and bits of conversation coming in waves from a window before falling into a deep slumber.

Those who could afford to were leaving the country. Most had to stay and continue their lives in the midst of uncertainty, without work or food. Those who managed to feed a couple of chickens in their backyard could at least eat eggs. Whoever had relatives in outposts like Çeşme packed their bags and moved there. Çeşme was at the tip of the peninsula of Izmir; the closest one could get to the island of Chios while remaining on land. The fear of displacement was already displacing people. Constantine closed his tavern. He had run it for twenty-six years. As he bolted the doors and boarded up the windows, he was blinded with tears. His wife was there and Polycarp, carrying food and sacks of flour out of the place. Whatever was deemed valuable or perishable was taken to the house. The floor of the old tavern creaked in protest every time they walked back and forth. It was a sound they were not used to hearing, as it had never been so quiet in there before. There used to be people at all hours, and on quiet mornings the noises from the port kept them company. Not any more.

"We'll come back and reopen it, Constantine," Carmela said, a little too enthusiastically. "We're not saying adieu; simply au revoir, right?" She looked at Polycarp as if asking for his help.

"Hmm," he replied unhelpfully, "if you say so . . . ," and proceeded to drag a sack of flour down the pavement into the horse cart. "Au revoir, big gutter rats in the wine cellar!" He waved at the old building mockingly. "Are we ready to go?"

Husband and wife took one last melancholy look at their tavern, then got into the back of the horse cart.

"Look at it this way," said Polycarp, "you might never fight again."

Uncle Constantine frowned in annoyance but said nothing. They remained silent the rest of the way, listening to the monotonous clip-clopping of the hooves, watching the unforgiving September luminosity oppress the streets. Light did not embrace the objects it touched, nor did it ooze around them with hues of yellow like in the summer. It was austere, penetrated the world with efficient precision to bring out the cold brownness in things.

"This is why the ancients called the place Ionia," Polycarp thought aloud, "everything is about light here." He spoke without realizing it.

"Huh?" said Carmela, nudged out of her thoughts by her nephew's voice. This happened often with Polycarp. He blurted things that had no apparent connection to the moment, as if he was having a conversation with someone invisible. The strange thing was that Marie, Elena, and little Niko all functioned the same way and seemed to follow each other's monologues. Strange birds indeed. She thought her infertility may have been God's way of preventing the strangeness of the family from being perpetuated. It was the first time she had had such a thought, and in the midst of her sadness it shone a glimmer of satisfaction.

"What was that you said?" she repeated.

"I was just thinking out loud . . . " Polycarp shrugged.

She insisted, "Was it something about light?"

"Almost autumn, isn't it?" Polycarp was now annoyed at having to translate a passing thought into an insignificant comment about the weather.

"Yes, indeed. How time flies . . . " she smiled.

"That means we're getting closer to the moment of our death," continued Polycarp. "Do you ever wonder about it? Will there be some twitching, will the heart just stop beating, will you agonize as you clutch onto one more second of breathing?"

Carmela opened her eyes wide in horror. "Shh. Be quiet, son! What kind of talk is this?"

"I thought you wanted to talk about time flying . . . "

She huffed, swinging her black curls, and looked for a wooden surface on which to knock. She knocked three times on a stool that was stacked beside her. "For heavens' sake Pol, can a person never have a normal conversation with you?"

"I don't know," he said softly, gazing absently above her head. Constantine, who had remained quiet since their departure from the tavern, pressed his wife's hand. "We're all anxious with everything that is happening these days." It was not Constantine's way to smooth out conversations gone awry. He seemed to have surprised himself in the act. He looked at his nephew and wife with half a smile, as if expecting congratulations. They paid no attention, and he nodded to himself, looking down between his knees at the wooden floor of the cart.

Kemal's army was coming and the Greeks had lost the war, everyone had figured this out. What no one knew was how it would affect Smyrna and its Rum population, the Levantines and Armenians. This was Constantine's worry, he could not begin to imagine being anywhere else but in Smyrna. He thought that having enough food for a few weeks and barricading themselves in the house would be sufficient. It had been, when the Greeks occupied Smyrna. His cousin's house was in Bayrakli, on the hills across from Smyrna. They could all bundle some belongings and wait it out there. A perfect solution. He would discuss it at home later.

The horse cart turned the corner into Marie's street. Polycarp noticed the open windows to Manolis's house and stood up, unable to contain his agitation.

"Someone's there!" He turned around and jumped out awkwardly from the back, stretching his legs over the upturned furniture on his way. He ran to Manolis's house, climbed the front steps two at a time, and hit the bronze knocker a few times while trying also to peek through the windows. He waited a while, knocked again. "Is anyone there?" he shouted into the window. "Manolis?"

A shadow moved deep in the house. "Who is that?" shouted Polycarp again, his voice trembling a little. It crossed the hallway one more time. Polycarp imagined an armed burglar and retreated a little. The door finally creaked open into a slit. Pol did not move forward, convinced a stranger would lunge out with a knife. A few seconds of silence later, there was more creaking. A man with a bushy black beard and tired eyes appeared at the entrance. Not lunging. Just standing there. Pol did not recognize the face.

The stranger recognized his.

"Pol . . . We meet again." He squinted, managed a smile.

"Mano . . . Dear God, what have they done to you?" Polycarp moved forward to embrace him. Manolis accepted his embrace, pulling back quickly. "I just arrived. Haven't shaved." Pol was not going away. "Come in. It's very dusty everywhere . . . Come, sit here."

Manolis pulled out a chair in the kitchen, by the window. They sat face to face, a wide sun ray crossing their faces as it fell on the tile floor. Manolis saw Pol's eyes with the sun in them for the first time. They were greenish, the brown washed away by sunlight. He did not say anything. Pol felt awkward. He used to mock Manolis mercilessly about his starched shirts and curly moustache, he remembered with some regret. The man looked like ruins now.

"When did you come back?"

"A few hours ago. By train. I was sleeping when I heard your voice . . . " He paused and then asked: "How is the family?"

"Fine. Good. Living at my uncle's for a while. Would you like to come over there, have a bite to eat? You must be hungry."

He kept looking at Manolis, trying to find what had changed, or rather, what had not. He looked hollow. Something eaten from inside, leaving the thinnest of surfaces, almost transparent, threatening collapse.

"I don't want to see anyone. Or talk."

"I'll bring you food then." Polycarp rose. "I'll come by in an hour. Wait for me. I won't stay if you don't want me to. Will you be here?"

Manolis nodded, looking away.

Pol walked out of the house, waving his hand at his old friend, as if asking for assurance he would be there upon his return.

Manolis remained seated at the kitchen chair unable to rise, his loose clothes falling off the sides of his body, his legs bony underneath the fabric, his shoulders slouched. He told himself it was time to get up, shave. He did not budge. Perhaps time was all that was left now. Was it? The kind that crushes you like a slab of concrete. He was a prisoner of immeasurable time. He wanted to weep but could not. Chios? Samos? His plans seemed immaterial, because he could not even get up from a chair. He wondered what he would do if someone broke his door down and came at him with a weapon. Would his legs gather up on their own and run?

The sun had moved. The kitchen looked abandoned in that state of imminent darkness, with his silhouette remaining immobile, like the rest of the furniture.

There are moments like this in childhood, he mused. You walk into a room drained of light and someone is sitting by the window. Someone in black with white hair. Your old grandmother who cannot see or hear. You see that profile with its creases and wrinkles but it does not move. She is holding her head with one small hand and not looking anywhere, simply is there by the window, which represents life for her, and she is always to be found at that spot until it is too dark and someone remembers to move her to bed.

Bamya Fields

A PINKISH SUNRISE GLOWS over the bamya fields, slanting over the stream gurgling on the side among the laurel bushes. The smell of fresh water spreads in the air as it flows over rocks and meanders around larger ones. Sergeant Ahmet hears a rooster in the distance as he moves towards the fields on his brown Arabian horse. He lightly caresses its flank as the animal ambles slowly, swaying its thick tail. Up the hill is a small house surrounded by poplars. Heaven, he thinks, must be someplace like this. He enjoys these small excursions in the countryside around the areas where they camp. For reconnaissance, officially. But for him it's a respite from the soldiers, the barked orders, the smell of blood and gunpowder. He stops the horse and gets off to wash his face in the stream. He kneels down and sticks his hands in the glacial water, then plunges his entire head into it suddenly, on impulse. He releases an "Aaah!" as he draws himself up, cold water trickling down his face onto his uniform. He plunges his head in again and rubs his face with his hands. When he pulls himself up he squeezes the water off his hair and rubs his neck. The horse starts drinking beside him, its hind legs occasionally moving to chase off the insects. Sergeant Ahmet unbuttons his jacket and takes it off, proceeds to take his shirt off. He kneels again to wet his chest, scrub his armpits. He walks around in small circles waiting for his chest to dry before he can wear his uniform again. Peace, he thinks. Quiet, at last. He puts on his shirt and his jacket and khaki cap. He pats the side of the horse, who comes away from the stream, and waits for his master to mount him. He does not, though. He walks beside his horse, his hand on the animal's flank.

Sergeant Ahmet discovers flowering capers on the side of the dusty road. White, with purple centers and long thin pistils. He did not know a caper was a budding flower. Never saw it before. As he walks on he comes across a piece of red cloth. Not dusty, rather clean. He pulls it out from the tall, dried-up yellow grass and finds a child's blouse. A girl's, with a round-edged collar; the size of a seven-year-old, perhaps. Hard to tell. A little smaller than his own. Ceylan. He sees his own child's face among the capers and shudders. The buttons look torn. Torn buttons, not good, he thinks, heart starting to quicken. He walks into the thick grass. There is a hand. A small hand, with blood on the fingertips, like henna. The palm is relaxed. He pushes aside the grass and finds the arm, and then the rest of the girl who is lying with eyes open and glazed with death, naked. On her white abdomen there are smudges of blood, and between her legs a pool of it. He closes his eyes, feeling faint. His fingers dig into his palm through the red blouse. He walks away and collapses into the grass, vomiting. He knows there must be more and he should look for them. He knows he should hurry and get some men to bury the bodies. He does not know if he has a voice left to speak. He feels it retreating into a deep dark place underneath his throat and tries to swallow it, to push it even further down, where no one will ever find it.

He finds them all. The old woman, the old man, and his son. They are scattered around the field, all with eyes wide open. The son looks different somehow. There is something about him that doesn't quite fit in with the place, but it is not the clothing. It is not the moustache. There is something too polished about him, but he cannot tell why. Then he looks at the hands. The long bony fingers, the smooth palms bruised from recent work. These are not peasant hands. These are hands that used pens, held books. Sergeant Ahmet marvels how they ended up here, in this bamya field. Flies are buzzing over the corpses, sitting on the noses or the hair indiscriminately. He runs up to the house on the hill. The door is wide open. They were dragged out at night. The table is still covered with crumbs, the dirty plates are stacked. They had just finished eating. He feels a sudden pain in his chest. Crouches on the floor again, unable to breathe, gasping for air. He can't help imagining the scenes. Tries to narrow his thoughts down. Need blankets to cover them. He pulls sheets, blankets, whatever he can rip off the beds and runs back out. He kneels beside the child, pulling a cover over her limp white body; gathers her arms close to her on her sides. She has a tiny chest, the size of an open hand. He wants to caress her hair, like a father who puts a child to sleep, to ease something, the horror that remained imprinted there after the fact. He brushes the softness of the silky black curls and pulls the blanket over her blank face quickly. His cheeks move up into his eyes, making a grimace of pain. Sergeant Ahmet wants to tear his own face off, but it is only this grimace he manages as he implodes into silent sobs.

A Case of the Runs

ALL NIGHT LONG ELENA lay awake listening to the dull persistent echoes from far away, blasts, echoes, thuds from the war now finally entering Smyrna. They had already boarded up the windows and doors, bracing for what appeared to be the final battle, here in the city, between the retreating Greek forces and the Turkish army in pursuit. The sounds terrified her in the dark. She imagined Nazım among the soldiers; she hoped that she would see him again. A shiver went through her as she thought of him. Then another, at the thought that she might never see him again. Manolis had returned and would see no one, sitting in the darkness of his house. She planned to go and convince him to join them. He would be safer. Tomorrow, she said to herself, I'll go get him. I'll wake up early and go get him. Among the thuds and blasts she thought she heard voices far away. Something like a continuous hum that got louder steadily. She sat up in her bed, heart beating fast. I have to wake them up, she thought. Get them up and be ready. She opened her door and found them all there, standing in the hallway, looking anxious, trying to understand the danger they were in. The sounds of the war were still quite far, which meant they had enough time to leave the house. Constantine's house was close to the Quay where most of the consulates were. They could seek refuge in one of them. The Italian. "We should get dressed," Elena's voice came out evenly. Niko kept searching the adults' faces for answers. He kept having flashes, memories from the time they had gone looking for his uncle on the Quay, among the crowds and the shooting. He did not want to leave. "I'm scared," he said.

Constantine ignored the child's cry. "I was thinking of going to Bayrakli," he said, "cousin Adelia's house on the hills. Safer to be there than here."

"What about my house? My furniture, my carpets?" whined Carmela.

"What about your life?" Pol responded curtly.

Carmela looked around mournfully. "At least the Bukhara carpet . . . We can fold it and the men can carry it." Constantine and Pol looked at each other. Constantine put his foot down. "We're just carrying some food and essentials. We'll return in a few days, anyway, when everything is calmer." Niko looked at the pyjama-clad adults discussing departure.

"I'm getting dressed," he said.

He went back to his room. The adults became silent and followed suit.

Constantine instructed the women to wear all their jewellery under their clothes, the rings around chains so they would not be visible. They should also wear layers of clothes so that they carried as little as possible. When finally they were dressed, all looking well padded, Carmela went to the kitchen to fill up empty wine bottles with water and small bags with food for each to carry. Before departure, she stared at her Bukhara carpet mournfully. "It was a wedding gift from my aunt," she explained to Niko, loud enough for her husband to hear her. "God rest her soul . . . She raised me, you know. I was an orphan too." She caressed the boy's hair. "When you grow up, I would like you to have it," she continued. "It will be a souvenir from me and your uncle."

An hour later, they were walking down the street, Constantine and Polycarp carrying the Bukhara carpet rolled into an enormous cylinder. The sun had risen above the horizon, its orange reflections gleaming from the limestone walls and red tiles of the roofs. It was relatively quiet in the side streets. Most houses had their shutters closed and their doors boarded up.

Constantine said to his wife, who followed behind him, without turning his head, "Do you think we can run or hide with this enormous thing you're making us carry?"

Polycarp, who was ahead of his uncle, smiled to himself. Here they were, trying to make a furtive exit with a huge sausage on their shoulders. Carmela did not respond to her husband's comment. She did not want to make a spectacle on the street. She knew he was right, but could not bring herself to part from the thing. It was her inheritance; she could not fathom why it tugged at her heart so. Being an orphan meant feeling unsafe in the world most of the time. Her spinster aunt used to threaten to put her in an orphanage whenever she was mad at her, and that was often. She remembered opening her eyes every morning, wondering if this might be the day. She peed on this carpet once. She was made to scrub it. Some days, she lay on it, inhaling the woolly smell and daydreaming. All those moments came to her now, walking in the almost deserted sidestreets, not knowing if she'd ever return home. The husband can complain all he wants, she thought; this Bukhara goes wherever I go.

"We should join a crowd that's going towards the Italian Consulate. We'll be safe," she offered. Constantine tried to turn his head towards her and bumped his face into the carpet and exclaimed, "Oh? Why didn't we think of it before? Tell me, dearest, which crowd do you prefer?" He gestured at the deserted street in annoyance as he swayed back and forth under his load.

Carmela was not fazed. "We'll soon enter the avenue, I'm sure there are a lot of people there."

Her husband grumbled unintelligibly.

Niko felt his intestines tighten. He squeezed all his muscles, trying to make the pain go away. He felt desperate and after a few more steps said, "I need to go to the bathroom."

"Oh, ghamota!" grumbled Constantine. "Just pee beside that tree."

"It's number two."

"Porca miseria!" Constantine turned back suddenly without warning and the roll of carpet went flying off his shoulder. "Are we ever going to get away from here? Does anyone else need something?"

Elena, who had been quiet until then, walked up to Polycarp and took the carpet from him.

"Just take him back to the house and lock up afterwards, that's all."

Polycarp nodded, taking Niko by the hand. The child's palm was cold and clammy. He suddenly remembered Spinoza. He had forgotten the bird. He did not say anything as he rushed his nephew down the street.

"We're going straight ahead, you'll catch up with us," Constantine shouted behind them.

In the dark bathroom, Niko sat, shivering. He felt his guts loosen and contract at unexpected intervals, so that he was unable to gauge when to get up and be done. He sat, sweat gathering on his forehead, waiting. Polycarp's steps around the house reassured him. His hands were trembling as he finally pulled up his pants. I am always afraid, he realized. I am always sweating, shaking and shitting, thinking they will kill us. Will I ever stop being afraid? Will this ever pass?

"Are you done, Niko?" asked Polycarp.

Niko opened the door.

"Your face is the colour of chalk, child . . . "

Niko stood there, trembling.

"Sit here," Polycarp guided him towards a chair, holding the candle he had lit high above the child's head. Niko sat gathering his knees up to his stomach. Polycarp put the canary cage on the table next to Niko. "Almost forgot him. See, thanks to your diarrhea, we came back to get Spinoza."

Niko tried to nod. He was in no state to think about the bird.

Polycarp rattled on, "If Aunt Carmela can take her carpet, we can take our bird, n'est-ce pas?"

Niko felt his guts tighten again and ran to the bathroom.

A few minutes later his uncle was scrutinizing his face, holding the candle close. "You're looking fine now. Take this."

He handed him the bird cage and led him towards the door. He blew out the candle and they were outside. Niko was still feeling weak but Polycarp assured him he looked fine. They had already spent half an hour in the house while the others were advancing.

"Now we'll walk fast, we can even run a bit until we get to the avenue and then the Quay. It'll bring colour to your cheeks too. Try not to move the bird too much." They started walking hurriedly down the street, Niko making efforts not to shake Spinoza's cage. Polycarp kept glancing sideways at his nephew until he was satisfied the boy was no longer sick with fear, holding the big cage awkwardly in his arms as he hurried along.

There were people everywhere now, going in groups towards the Quay. Many carried suitcases, the men of one family were carrying the grandmother on a chair tied to long wooden rods. The ancient woman kept crossing herself and moving her lips silently in prayer.

It would be difficult to find the rest of the family, Polycarp realized as they became stuck in the crowd. He tried slowly to squeeze his way towards the Italian Consulate, looking back frequently to make sure his nephew was nearby. When they finally reached the Consulate, the entrance was crowded with people trying to push their way in, waving their papers and being pushed back by gendarmes telling them to get in line.

Polycarp felt trapped. He could not hear anything. He took the bird cage from Niko and told him to climb on his shoulders to see if he could see the rest of the family in the crowd. Niko climbed on his uncle's shoulders and looked all around, squinting his eyes to see farther.

"Look for the carpet," Pol suggested.

That's when he felt it coming.

He had to put it off. He had to take care of the boy. He closed his eyes to calm himself, wondering if for once he could overcome it through sheer willpower. It rose from depths he could not even fathom. It rose gradually like a numbness spreading through his veins. He wanted to run, disappear. "I think I see them," shouted Niko, "over there!"

"Can you go?" he asked.

"Not without you!"

"Take me there, then."

His hand grew limp in Niko's grasp. The boy knew immediately. "Don't let go of me, uncle. I need you!"

"Yes . . . "

They pushed through the crowd, Niko ahead of his uncle, one hand stretched out to push people aside, the other gripping his uncle's hand so it would not slip away.

"We're almost there," he said as he pulled on Polycarp's arm.

Polycarp let himself be carried along, holding the bird cage with one hand. He was feeling cut off from everything. His world was coming unglued. Niko knew exactly. These were the times his uncle walked out of the house in pyjamas only to return days later. Sometimes he didn't. He was found by someone on the street somewhere, smelling of urine and feces, head filled with lice. They all lived in fear of such moments. That he would leave and never find his way back. There had been talk of interning him at the Hopital de la Paix in Constantinople, where nuns would look after him, but his grandmother had always refused.

It was as if Polycarp would just let go of everything and float away, like a small boat breaking loose from its ropes, into rough seas. Sometimes he argued by himself wandering through the streets, pulling people to their windows, smiling. "It's just Marie's crazy son. Look! Jacob's orphan is trying to get him back to the house!" Niko knew he and his uncle had titles. He pushed past the massive adults, all huddled together like a soft wall, advancing and retreating in unison to get into the Consulate. His arm was hurting.

"Uncle, try to walk, I cannot pull you like this. My arm's going to fall off!"

Polycarp was not listening. He was gazing blankly at a spot high above. It was as though he had frozen into a statue of himself. Niko was growing discouraged. What appeared a short distance was turning out to be a very long one. But at least his uncle was not screaming and shouting nonsense. At least he was moving along when he could.

They reached the rest of the family. Marie wept at the sight of them, mumbling prayers of gratitude. Constantine suggested they try to break out of the crowd and walk out of the city without consular protection. His wife thought it too risky.

"I'm going," said Polycarp with an air of finality. He raised the bird cage up in front of his face and started going away, pushing through the crowds.

"Where are you going?" shouted his mother with alarm. "I have to get away," he replied, waving. "So long!"

"Going where?"

"I'll meet you later." He waved, pushed his way through and disappeared.

"Constantine, do something!" Marie was frantic.

Constantine tried to follow Polycarp.

"Come back here!" shouted his wife. "We can't lose you too!"

Constantine returned. Elena's eyes kept searching the crowd in the direction her brother had left. She told Niko to climb on her shoulders. Constantine hauled him on his back. Niko searched the crowd and shook his head no. Elena covered her eyes, her shoulders shaking. She wept like this, in angry silence. Her aunt tried to pat her back and was pushed away.

Finally she wiped her tears with her sleeve and said, "I'll go find him."

Marie did not know whether to hold her back or send her off.

Niko jumped in, "He won't want to come. He's not well."

"He'll wander around and get killed!" Elena snapped.

"How are you going to make him come back?"

"It's pointless to wait here, in this huge crowd anyway!" Elena retorted. "What are we waiting for exactly?"

"Shall we go back home and lock ourselves up?" asked Constantine wearily.

No one liked the idea. Elena started pushing through the crowd without further consultation.

"Do something, Constantine!" his wife scolded.

"What do you want me to do? She's not a child . . . "

Niko followed his aunt.

"Fine!" said Constantine to his wife. "You want your carpet? Hold the other end!"

They all followed Elena in a serpentine line, searching for Polycarp in the thickening crowd.

Everyone is waiting, Niko observed. The war has entered the city and everyone is waiting here. They don't want to wait at home, they come out here, where they can smell each other and huddle. They pile up by the sea. Will they swim away?

Warships were quietly picking up people and leaving the bay. Foreigners mostly. Those who did not need to wait at the entrances of the Consulates. The rest had to make lines here and there in front of buildings, hoping for protection, waving papers that attested to some claim of nationality, albeit slim. Meanwhile, Elena led her family away from all this, inch by inch, elbowing her way out of the crowd. She figured Polycarp could not be very far away, having had to do the same thing.

She did not have a plan, except that she must find her brother. How she would convince him to stay with them was another matter, but she wanted to prevent his wandering off amidst looters and soldiers. None of them was thinking too much of the danger they were facing, although there were occasional screams now and loud explosions coming from inside the city. They encountered American officers patrolling the streets, which reassured them. They asked about Polycarp, but no one had seen him. They tried to walk towards familiar places that he might have sought, without success. They wandered in large avenues only, where they were able to see some gendarmes. They ate their food and drank all their water, finally realizing there was nothing left to do but walk towards Bayrakli, to cousin Adelia's house, without Polycarp.

Then the sun sank splendidly, the way an enormous juicy orange rolls off a blue tablecloth, and Niko thought of his uncle, who told him stories about Ios. Stories from long ago, invented by people who were dazzled by the very same sunset over the Smyrnian bay, here in Ionia. Whether the earth shook and destroyed the city countless times or Lame Timur came to have pyramids constructed with chopped human heads for his pleasure, the gods' chariots always crossed this very sky to give the sun its rest, unsullied by human strife. Beauty remained. The gods were all around, Niko felt with a shudder. He wondered if he would ever see his uncle again. This sunset on this day, he knew, would somehow define his life. It would return to haunt his soul. Beauty seemed neither cruel nor good. It was oblivious. It would not kneel for anyone. And this, he reflected, you figured in such privileged moments of suffering and fear, as you prayed to remain alive.

It happened hours later as they walked along the sea shore, already outside the city's core. First, there was an explosion that shook the ground, followed by others. Then they saw plumes of black smoke rise from the city across the bay. They continued walking until they reached the top of a hill.

"Smyrna is burning!" Carmela exclaimed.

They stood gaping at the spreading fire filling the horizon with thick black smoke.

Marie crossed herself.

Later, they heard the stories. People jumping off the Quay into the water, swimming towards ships whose captains had refused to board them. Those who got to them were pushed off and drowned. Those who did not find a boat or a ship to take them swam until they could no more. Suitcases floating, their flaps open, clothes scattered. Families running away from the fire and into the arms of thugs who slit their throats. Screaming. Mothers wailing, pressing their dead children to their bosoms. The fire extending all the way to the sea, lighting up the bay, red hot beams falling from skeletal houses on top of crowds. People roasting and howling unable to reach the water. Small children dead from thirst long before the flames ate their small bodies. The smell of burnt flesh, burnt lives. Bodies rotting in doorways, side streets, avenues; bludgeoned, disfigured, massacred by frenzied mobs. Foreign officers on their ships, writing reports. Correspondents in cabins typing up headline stories for newspapers elsewhere. Admirals in their unwrinkled uniforms sending urgent telegrams.

The fire ran its course, having scorched—it seemed—everything except the water. Those whose lives were spared lived in unharmed quarters, or outside the city, and could not tell the stories of horror. The few who did survive spent their lives regretting it. They told the stories they could not bear to remember, until they were heard no more.

Much later, began the story-laundering. Official versions of who did what to whom. From both sides of the Aegean came stories of glory and bitterness that only children believed. It was, of course, meant for them.

Niko's uncle never returned. Niko heard much later from his friend Alexa that able-bodied fathers, sons, brothers were marched out of the city and shot, if they were Rum, or could not prove otherwise. Her father and brothers were, but they could not prove otherwise, so she was orphaned. Niko wondered if his uncle was among them, taken away for a mistaken identity like his father.

Another story they heard was that hospitals were abandoned on the day of the fire. The nuns left patients lying in their beds to await their fate without food or water; and those who could run were let loose in the burning city in their bed clothes; the nuns boarded the foreign ships and went away. Niko imagined pyjama-clad fools running amok, much like his uncle used to, but these were pursued by flames, disoriented, having nowhere to go except into the arms of thugs, or into the vast sea that swallowed bodies only to spit them once it had sucked out their souls. There were so many floating cadavers in the harbour that it took days to clean up, they said.

Weeks later Constantine returned to the city alone, to estimate the damage. His house was gone, so was his sister's. A hole gaped where Manolis's house used to be. Constantine wondered whether he burned to death sitting in his chair or whether he had managed to escape on a boat. He looked for Polycarp, walking furtively in streets that were beyond recognition, filled with rubble and twisted iron. Many of the schools had burned down, so had the hospitals and churches. There was very little left except for skeletons of buildings, half-eaten facades with walls covered in soot, carbonized beams sticking out over the streets. Soldiers were patrolling the debris. The smell of putrefaction lingered.

He went to St Polycarp's Church and found it intact, although the surrounding area had completely burned to the ground. He was less likely to shout "Miracle!" than his wife Carmela. She would certainly start a myth about how St Polycarp saved his church if he told her; still, he felt awe at witnessing something so mysterious. He pushed open the tall iron door of the churchyard and smelt a whiff of the honeysuckle drooping in heavy boughs along the wall. Then his breath left him. He stood there paralyzed. On the ground, among the tree trunks and shrubs stood Polycarp's bird cage, empty, its tiny door wide open. Constantine's heart was beating furiously as he knocked on the church door. He knocked until he heard a faint, nasal voice asking who was there in French. He responded in French and the friar opened the door reluctantly, sticking his pointy face out, and sized up Constantine.

"What can I do for you?" the friar asked, his head tilted sideways.

"I am looking for my nephew, Polycarp. Is he here? This bird cage is his." He pointed vaguely at it.

The friar nodded and opened the door wider.

"A thin man with curly black hair and large eyes?" he asked. His hands were plump and moved in flourishes.

"That's he!" replied Constantine, excited.

"He was in the yard during the fire. Wouldn't come inside. He sat there with his bird cage. Kept talking to Spinoza. We figured he must have been a little . . . " he moved his meaty hand as if screwing a bulb next to his temple " . . . eccentric . . . "

"What happened to him?"

"I brought him food and kept begging him to come in. He ate but would not budge. He just kept talking. To himself, since Spinoza has been dead for some centuries . . . " He tried to prevent a furtive and slightly pedantic smile, moving his bald head sideways.

Constantine suppressed an urge to pull the friar by the collar and shake the information out of him.

"Spinoza is the name of the canary," he cut in impatiently.

"Ah?" The friar raised his eyebrows. "I see . . . Well, as I was saying, he refused to come in. Luckily no marauders attacked him. The gate has no lock, you see. But he disappeared yesterday. I came out in the morning to bring him food and the cage was empty, just like this. He was gone."

Constantine's heart sank.

The friar added, "Perhaps he is looking for you?"

"Hmm . . . " Constantine was not convinced.

"What to do now?" he asked, feeling sad.

"If you give me your address, I'll tell him where to find you, should he ever come back. Or try to bring him to you, if he lets me . . . "

Constantine wrote the address on a piece of paper. He thanked the friar and left the churchyard, shoulders downcast. A few moments later he returned, picked up the bird cage, and left.

For years after, the family remained in a state of mournful anticipation. Every knock on the door made them jump. Whenever they walked around the city, they expected to run into him. For years, in fact, until her death, Marie refused to speak of her son in the past tense. Niko felt orphaned once again, having lost the uncle who was so close to him.

Elena never painted again. Her copy of *Dulle Griet* had turned to ashes and did not make it into Van der Meer's collection, the latter having left the country, never to be heard of again. Deep in her heart she associated her depiction of *Dulle Griet* with the destruction of Smyrna and her personal tragedy. She took to spending her days sitting by a window, looking out vaguely with the melancholy eyes of someone who did not expect to find much out there, yet could not stand what remained inside.

Of Niko's childhood, no proof remained except for the Bukhara carpet. There were no photographs, no identity papers, or birth registers. It was as if his existence had entirely vanished in the flames. Just like the city itself, he reconstructed his life randomly, carefully moving away from his past. He painted, like his aunt once had, but depicted abstractions. He went nowhere near his childhood all his life. He rarely strolled along the Quay; every time he did, bits of his past ripped into the placid scenery, pulling him away from his life. He saw the girl in her Sunday dress, sitting dead, with blood oozing around her wide open eyes, the fez that rolled on the pavement when the head that went with it crashed down like a watermelon that breaks open, Emine Hanım's slipper flying into the street when she got kicked by a thug, his grandmother sitting on the cold tiles holding a rifle she did not know how to use, his uncle walking away with the bird cage, his father waving from the train in his underwear. It was as if a nightmare came crawling over his waking life, threatening to take over. He avoided the Quay, even though, just like in the old days, all the roads in Izmir meant to take you there. The woman he married was from elsewhere and his children grew up without stories.

Loren Edizel was born in Izmir, Turkey. Her other works include the novel *Adrift* (TSAR, 2011) and several stories, including "The Conch," which appeared in Turkish translation in the anthology *Izmir in Women's Stories* (Kadın Öykülerinde Izmir). *The Ghosts of Smyrna* was published as *Izmir Hayaletleri* in Turkey in 2008 by Senocak Yayinlari (trans. Roza Hakmen). She lives in Toronto.